Books by Fairfax Downey

CAVALRY MOUNT

ARMY MULE

JEZEBEL THE JEEP

DOG OF WAR

WAR HORSE

INDIAN-FIGHTING ARMY

DISASTER FIGHTERS

PORTRAIT OF AN ERA, AS DRAWN BY C. D. GIBSON

RICHARD HARDING DAVIS—HIS DAY

BURTON, ARABIAN NIGHTS ADVENTURER

THE GRANDE TURKE

YOUNG ENOUGH TO KNOW BETTER

WHEN WE WERE RATHER OLDER

FATHER'S FIRST TWO YEARS

A COMIC HISTORY OF YALE

CAVALRY MOUNT

BY

FAIRFAX DOWNEY

ILLUSTRATED BY

PAUL BROWN

DODD, MEAD & COMPANY
NEW YORK 1946

PRINTED IN THE UNITED STATES OF AMERICA
BY THE VAIL-BALLOU PRESS, INC., BINGHAMTON, N. Y.

To Sally Ann Hall

FOREWORD

THOUGH written in 1929, the following words * of Lt. Gen. James G. Harbord, U.S.A., whose fine military career included service in the cavalry from 1891 to 1914, seem still well worth quoting in 1946:

> We shall be well advised as a nation if we do not depend too seriously upon peace pacts, nor listen too confidingly to the hum of the airplane or the siren song of the temperamental aviator, nor yet to those who believe the robot can replace the soldier and that armies are to be completely mechanized. There is still need for the cavalryman and his horse.

* An excerpt from his introduction to *The Horse of the Desert* by William Robinson Brown. New York, 1929. Quoted by permission.

Oh, pray for the soldier, you kind-hearted stranger.
He has roamed o'er the prairie for many a year.
He has kept the Comanches from off your ranches,
And chased them far over the Texas frontier.

EPITAPH ON THE GRAVE OF AN
UNKNOWN SOLDIER, FORT CLARK, TEXAS.

CONTENTS

ILLUSTRATIONS

1: BLACK HORSE WITH WHITE LEG

I

He was black as night, except for his near foreleg with its "stocking" of gleaming white, so short it might almost be called a sock. He stood a little over fifteen hands high, and his conformation was good though a trifle short-coupled. But the feature of the horse that caught and held your eye was his crest.

Crest was the word for that proudly-arched neck and head held high. His eyes were alight with spirit and intelligence. His ears, pricked up alertly, were small and set rather close together. Had his mane been roached, his crest would have been the very image of the horse heads the ancient Greeks sculptured, or of the black knight of a chess set. Somehow, you could not picture him as ever crestfallen.

The horse, led by a lanky, loose-jointed man through the single street of a frontier town to be watered in the stream beyond, stepped springily and tossed his head. Men turned to look at him.

It was curious that he should attract any attention. In the Texas Panhandle in 1870, only extraordinary horses drew more than a passing glance. Thousands of wild horses still roamed the plains. Blooded stock whirled the Concord coaches over the stage routes, and fine animals were to be found in many emigrant trains. A fiery palomino stallion, newly roped in a wild horse hunt, or a sleek Kentucky thoroughbred might win admiring scrutiny, but certainly not a small, black gelding. Perhaps it was the horse's bearing and his air of lively interest in his surroundings and the people along the street which caused them, in turn, to notice him.

And it was evident that the lanky man leading the black meant him to be noticed. His air of unconcern was a shade too elaborate. After he had walked the length of the street, he appeared to recollect some pressing errand at the store at the other end. Swinging himself on to the horse's back, he trotted back to the store, slid off and entered while his mount stood patiently. The lanky man then emerged and rode back toward the stream. In the course of this performance he had succeeded in demonstrating that the black horse possessed not only a steady walk, an even trot, and a swinging canter, but a fast running walk and a smooth single-foot which made his rider seem to be comfortably seated on an air cushion. Here was a horse with five gaits.

A watching cowboy grinned at the show staged by the lanky man.

"Yankee hoss trader," he drawled and turned away.

But that impromptu horse show had not been put on in vain. When man and horse had passed, two spectators followed—a grizzled, gray-bearded major of cavalry and a stout, swarthy man, part Mexican, part Indian from his features. Twice, the latter's beady, black eyes had gleamed while he watched the horse. Once, in admiration of the smooth, single-footed gait and again—and brighter—at the sight of the horse's one white leg.

The major, quicker on his feet, reached the quarry first. Content to bide his time and put in the last bid, the prosperous-looking half-breed waited and covertly observed from a distance. The Army man strode to where the black horse was being watered and ran appraising eyes expertly over the animal. In the traditional manner he opened the bargaining.

"Fair little nag you've got there," he said. "Has some faults and defects, I see, but not a bad horse all in all. Morgan blood."

"Yep," the owner confirmed. "He's a Morgan hoss. Lot of Morgan in him. You can't miss it."

"You're right," the major agreed. Always had it amazed him how remarkably and faithfully the traits of the original Morgan sire had been passed on to his descendants. That little bay stallion, no more than fourteen hands high and weighing less than a thousand pounds, had been named Justin Morgan after the singing-master who owned him. On a Vermont farm he had hauled logs and plowed until his speed was discovered. Then he won so many races, both running and trotting, with prizes ranging from a gallon of rum to a purse of money, that he made himself and his owner famous. For more than twenty years he was kept at stud.

"Yes, you're right," the major repeated. "It's a strong strain. Justin Morgan was foaled about 1789, I think. After I don't know how many generations you can still tell his get. Bays, browns, chestnuts, and blacks, they've all got small, close-set ears like this fellow here and they hold their heads high and their eyes are fine. They've most of 'em got the endurance and courage and gentleness their sire Justin had."

"So they hev," the lanky man confirmed. "Naow all that ever got passed down in my fam'ly is this here long nose thet tuhns red come the fuhst cold spell."

"These horses make corking good cavalry mounts," the major mused aloud, paying no attention to the other. "Our regular cavalry rode Morgans and Morgan-thoroughbreds in the Mexican War. So did those of us who were lucky enough to get 'em in the Civil War. General Sherman rode a Morgan. Mine—and a grand little horse he was—was killed under me in the Wilderness."

"Back hum in Vermont," the lanky man observed, "there's a statue to the Morgan hoss. Hain't nary a gen'rul atop him neither. Jest the hoss. It's like you say, Major. Any man thet owns a Morgan hoss has a valu-able piece of propputty."

The cavalryman bit his lip. He suddenly realized that he, the buyer, had been giving a sales talk and bidding up an animal he wished to acquire. Well, it was too late now.

"Sell him?" he asked abruptly.

"Might," the Vermonter conceded. "Hain't anxious to, though. I'm a-movin' my fam'ly to Californiay. Need the hoss and he reminds us of hum."

"Horses are cheap in this country," the officer said gruffly. "I'll look this fellow over."

He patted the Morgan's smooth forehead. With deft fingers he parted lips wet from drinking and scanned the firm, even teeth. "Four-year-old," he remarked. Carefully, he ran practiced hands down the length of legs from knee or hock to fetlocks. He needed only to tap a leg, and the black politely raised that foot for the hoof to be examined.

"Mind walking and trotting him up and down a bit?" he requested.

The Morgan's owner put him through his paces. His action was rhythmical and at the end his breathing was deep and steady.

"Passed," the major declared approvingly. "I'll buy him for the Army." He named a sum.

The Vermonter only grinned and shook his head at the price offered.

"Can't bargain with you," the officer said shortly. "That's the top price the Army lets me pay. It's twice what I'm giving for plain mustangs. Better take it. Horses hereabouts are cheap and plentiful and buyers are apt to be scarce."

The horse's owner glanced pointedly toward the waiting half-breed. The man was richly dressed. Silver buttons glistened on his jacket.

Following the look, the officer snorted. "Think you've got a buyer in that *hombre?* That buzzard's a *Comanchero.*"

"What's thet?"

"A *Comanchero* is a fellow that trades with the Comanche Indians. Sells 'em firearms and whiskey like as not. Then they come whooping down on emigrants like you folks and lift your scalps."

"Got money, hain't he?"

"I don't doubt it." Abruptly, the major turned to go,

dusting his hands. Looking down at them, he saw a black stain on the palm with which he had felt the off foreleg of the black horse, wet from his having waded into the stream to drink.

"Say! You've dyed this animal's hide!" he accused.

"A mite mebbe," the Vermonter slyly admitted. "But no harm. He's sound like you seen. All I done was black three of his legs a tetch."

"Why, for the love of Heaven, did you do that?"

"Waal, Major, seein' as haow you wun't be a-tellin' no one, this's why. I missed a couple of fuhst-rate chances to sell this hoss 'count of the crazy notion some folks daown this way hev. They got it all pre-served in a pome. Heerd it enough to l'ahn it. Goes like this:

> " '*One white foot, buy him.*
> *Two white feet, try him.*
> *Three white feet, deny him.*
> *But if he's a hoss with four white feet,*
> *Hang him up for the crows to eat.*' "

"Rats!" the major snorted again. "So he's really got *four* white stockings and not just one, has he? Well, that won't bother me. I'll still buy him. You can find me in town if you don't sell him to that reptile over there. Hope for the horse's sake you don't."

The cavalryman briefly laid a caressing hand on the black horse's withers and walked rapidly away.

II

The swarthy man strolled over.

"*Señor,*" he greeted, "be with God."

"Haow be *you?*" the Vermonter responded.

"In good health," the other responded. "I am named

José Pieda Tafoya and I am a trader." He commenced the formula. "This animal appears to have some admirable qualities though he is not without a full measure of faults. Are you inclined to dispose of him?"

"Might. Sell or swap?"

"I have taken a mild and altogether unreasonable fancy to this horse. In my camp are two fine harness mules which I think you have seen. Foolish though it is, I will trade two mules for this one horse."

"Them two mewels!" The Vermonter, surprised by this handsome offer, recovered rapidly. "Waal, I'll be a loser but call it a swap."

He thrust the black's tie rope into the half-breed's hand. "He's yourn."

The *Comanchero* smiled an oily smile.

"The trade is made," he confirmed. "He will bring me luck—and I need it sorely—this black horse with one white leg. You, *señor,* doubtless are not aware that a *caballo* marked as is this one brings good fortune."

"Waal, I've heerd tell."

"It is true. There is an old saying among my people which proclaims it. It runs thus:

" '*If you have a horse with four white legs,*
Keep him not a day.
If you have a horse with three white legs,
Send him far away.
If you have a horse with two white legs,
Sell him to a friend.
If you have a horse with one white leg,
Keep him to the end.'

Si, it speaks true. But you need not believe it. In any event, the horse now is mine."

The lanky New Englander smothered a grin.

"So he be, Mister. He's yourn, white leg and all. Naow let's go git them mewels of mine."

III

The Morgan horse gave no sign of being aware of a change of ownership. Already in his young life he had changed hands half a dozen times. His initial training had been excellent. His treatment and care on the whole had been good. Men who had owned him had recognized his value as a piece of property, yet, as no more than that—not as a warm-blooded creature with spirit and emotions and affection.

A horse—some horses more than others, just as with human beings—has the need of receiving and bestowing affection. Such was this scion of the celebrated Justin Morgan. Seldom had he known affection or been able to return it. Once, back North, there had been a boy and a girl in an orchard by the roadside. They had fed him apples, petted him, made much of him. He had rubbed his soft muzzle against their cheeks and had never forgotten. With all children he was especially gentle.

But the black horse was not long in deciding that he did not care at all for this new master.

The *Comanchero* had broken camp and moved out that same morning. In Tafoya's outfit were two Conestoga wagons, drawn by mule teams, and a herd of about twenty mustangs, driven by two *vaqueros*. The stout owner elected to ride his new purchase. They cinched a heavy Mexican saddle tight on the Morgan and forced a cruel spade bit into his mouth. Up on his back, the *Comanchero* heaved his not inconsiderable bulk. He would permit only the single-foot. When the horse tried to rest himself by a change of gait, he felt the wrench of the bit and the raking of sharp-roweled spurs.

The train pushed on hard and fast, bound to make a safe camp that night for a trading rendezvous early the next morning with a band of Comanches. The Morgan was weary and sweat-streaked, but he carried on, his head still up.

Once they forded a river. They splashed through several stream beds.

Now, *Señor* José Pieda Tafoya was well known to the Comanches and to their cousins, the Kiowas—well and favorably known to most of the tribesmen with refuges and hunting grounds in and around the Staked Plain of Texas. Since he illicitly traded them goods they craved—guns and firewater—he could count on being welcome and reasonably safe in their country. Therefore, the fate that befell him, along toward evening, when his wagons dipped down into the arroyo chosen as a camping site, could truly be termed pure mischance—indeed the acme of ill fortune.

A party of Southern Cheyennes, raiding far south of their usual haunts, swooped down on the train. In a few minutes, *vaqueros* and teamsters had been shot or clubbed to death. Herd and mule teams stampeded. A bullet knocked the swarthy Tafoya out of his saddle. He hit the ground with a thud, one hand still convulsively clutching the reins. Even amid that wild whooping and yelling, the well-trained black horse stood still beside his fallen rider.

Through glazing eyes the swarthy man stared at the legs of the black horse he had bought for good luck. Dimly, but unmistakably, he perceived a startling alteration. Not simply one leg but all *four*—the dye washed out by the water through which they had passed—were *white!*

The *Comanchero's* last conscious thought was a line from the verse he had quoted that very morning:

> *"If you have a horse with four white legs,*
> *Keep him not a day."*

Now the howls of the Cheyennes, plundering the wagons and riding to round up the scattered herd, grew too much for the Morgan horse to bear. He jerked loose the reins from a stiffening hand, tossed his head and, black mane and tail streaming, galloped madly away through the dust clouds.

2: THE PRICE OF FREEDOM

I

FAST and furious was the black horse's gallop. There was panic and even delirium in his flight from the wild tumult back in the arroyo. The strange, terrifying smell of blood stung his flaring nostrils, and his ears still rang with fierce war whoops and the screams of dying men.

His hooves drummed a rapid tattoo on the prairie. Through it he heard the beat of other hooves, as the Cheyenne raiders raced in pursuit of the horses of the scattered herd. Like all fugitives, the Morgan was certain that he was the special quarry of every pursuer. Indeed two red warriors with lariats coiled for a throw did converge on him. They could have cut him off and roped him easily, but they were diverted by a fleeing pinto, its red hide marked with broad patches of white hair. Dearest to the savage heart were such gaudy "painted" ponies as this one. Without an instant's hesitation, the Cheyennes sped off after him, abandoning the Morgan, only a dull and unspectacular black.

But the coal-black horse did not realize he was being allowed to escape. In a frenzy he tried to redouble his speed. He snorted in terror and his eyes rolled wildly, as he thundered on at headlong pace.

A tenderfoot horse from the East, he had not yet learned the lessons of the prairie. At full gallop he stepped in a prairie dog hole.

At that pace, nine times out of ten he would have broken a leg. This time was the merciful tenth. The black hurtled forward, whirled head over heels in half a somersault. He lit with a crash square on his back. The high pommel of the heavy Mexican saddle partly broke his fall, but his weight crushed the saddle's wooden frame as if it were matchwood. Its girth burst as he slid ten feet ahead and lay inert, all his wind knocked out of him.

He lay still but not for long. Gasping and groaning, he struggled to his feet. Something held his head low. It was the loop of the reins, fallen over his head and pinned to the ground by his own forefeet resting on them. Dazed and still frightened, the horse jerked up his head to win free. The throatlatch—its leather was cracked—broke, and the bridle slid down over his ears. Out of his mouth dropped the cruel spade bit.

In ecstasy, in exultation, the black horse shook his head and all his sturdy body. So must prisoners feel when irons which have manacled them are struck from their limbs. Now he bore no mark of his bondage to man save for his horseshoes, and of them he was not conscious. Neighing in triumph, the black horse again bounded across the prairie.

But he was sore and bruised and weary from galloping. He heard no further sounds of pursuit. Soon he slowed to a trot—then to a walk. At length he halted and, ears pricked forward, fine eyes shining, gazed all about him.

On all sides stretched the Texas prairie, bright with yellow, purple, blue, and scarlet flowers—sunflowers, buttercups, field violets, marigolds, poppies. Nowhere was there any sign of man or his habitations. In that vast expanse was the air of freedom, and the Morgan horse breathed deep.

A breeze stirring his mane, he made a handsome picture standing immobile there, like the statue of his forebear, Justin. Bright-hued butterflies flitted around him. A drove of wild turkeys took wing, and the sun glistened on their plumage as on burnished steel. In the distance, the horse saw a herd of deer climbing up through the chaparral from the stream bed where they had drunk.

He trotted in that direction and slaked his thirst also at the stream. Contentedly, he began grazing on the luscious prairie grass. Having eaten his fill, he lay down and rolled in pure delight.

Dusk shaded slowly into night. A hush fell on the prairie and the calm and cool of a spring night. Here were peace and ease and freedom.

Suddenly, the black horse was miserably, achingly lonely.

II

It was into the Staked Plain—*El Llano Estacado* in the Spanish tongue—that the lonesome Morgan ranged in search of company. Its broad expanse of hundreds of miles, rich with buffalo grass and well watered by lakes and streams, once had been a wild horse paradise where mustangs by the thousand and tens of thousand roamed.

Their myriads were descendants of the war horses the Conquistadores had brought from Spain to the New World; of steeds escaped or strayed from armored columns of Cortez and Coronado, from pack trains and from settlements; of horses, stolen by the Indians in raids on ranch or hacienda or on the emigrant trains bound for California—horses lost in turn by the red men in stampedes or storms. These wild horses, interbreeding, mingled the blood of Spanish sires and Arab barbs with that of English and American thoroughbred strains. There was also Morgan blood, like the black horse's, in some of the mustangs.

The black would have encountered immense herds on this stamping ground a little more than a score of years ago. Now he searched for long, weary hours and found not one of his kind.

Wild horse herds had grown scarce by 1857 and now, in 1870, were fewer still, so rapidly had their numbers been depleted by capture or slaughter. Continually, white men and red rounded them up for mounts or killed them off for meat or wolf bait or simply as pests which trampled crops or enticed away tame stock, horses, and mules, to their wild, free life.

But, on the third day, the black Morgan was successful in his quest. Topping a rise in the rolling prairie, he beheld a herd of more than fifty horses in a draw below. The bright sunlight made their sleek hides iridescent. He saw golden bays, and bays with black manes and tails. Orange and saffron duns. Sorrels and red sorrels. Grays and blacks like himself. Dove-colored palominos and parti-colored pintos.

He neighed joyously and trotted toward them.

One of the herd stalked out to meet him.

Deeper black than the Morgan, his hide was like jet. Nowhere on him was there a white hair. His mane and tail were sable plumes. He was a tall horse, well over seventeen hands—to the Morgan he looked gigantic—but beautifully proportioned. All symmetry and poise and grace. As he advanced majestically, he seemed to be marching to the rhythm of barbaric music: blaring trumpets and crashing cymbals and throbbing kettledrums.

The Morgan, lost in admiration, halted to watch the stately approach. Relief from accumulated loneliness welled up in him. He nickered a greeting as plaintive and appealing as it was joyful.

But now he began to sense the menace in the bearing of the oncoming black stallion—the wide-dilated nostrils, the eyes seeming to flash fire, the wrathful thud of his hooves. This was the master of the herd. He would welcome no stranger except, perhaps, a mare as a new addition to his harem. Any others ventured this close to his domain at their peril.

The green horse from the East, caution forgotten in his lonesomeness, was suddenly aware of his danger. He whirled and ran for his life.

He was as fast as his forebear, but the black stallion overtook him as if he had spread a pair of mighty sable wings and swooped down like a huge hawk. He thundered up alongside. Like the dart of a hawk's beak, too, was the swift thrust of the stallion's head toward the neck of the horse he towered over. Sharp teeth bit as powerful jaws clamped closed.

The black stallion swooped down like a huge hawk

Only the thickness of his mane saved the Morgan. The stallion, getting his mouth full of it, was not able to bite on down deep into the flesh of the neck. He jerked a clump of the mane out by its roots and squealed with frustrated rage, shouldering hard against his victim, his head poised to dart again.

With a shudder of terror, the little black swung away. Agile on his feet, he doubled back like a jack rabbit. He had gained ten yards before his enemy could check and swing around.

It was a brief and futile respite. Now the snorting stallion was upon him again. Once more the fugitive turned and doubled. But this time the other was ready for that trick and countered it by a turn almost as sharp. His teeth scored a bloody groove along the Morgan's withers.

The little gelding was tiring. He knew he could not last much longer against such furious strength. Soon he would be down, struck by those sharp hooves, pounded and trampled until he moved no more. The black stallion was a killer.

But, abruptly, the big horse drew off and galloped away. The chase had taken the master far from his herd. In his absence some other stallion, lurking about for just such an opportunity, might run off his mares. Or young stallions he himself had driven out, once they had grown from colts into possible rivals, might slip back to cut out a few fillies for consorts.

The big black's anxiety for his mares was the Morgan's salvation. He stood not upon the order of his going but fled from that place until exhaustion slowed his pace. With heaving flanks, legs spread, at last he halted. Around him, disconsolate and alone, the prairie spread limitless.

III

Occasionally the black sighted small groups of wild horses, outcasts from the herds. Lonely though he was, he never attempted to discover whether they would let him join them. Too fresh in his mind was the dreadful memory of the sable stallion.

Once he beheld the brown, moving mass which was a herd of buffalo and trotted closer to investigate. Surprisingly, the big bull leader led the herd in flight from the single, unridden horse. Often had the herd been hunted and harried by men mounted on such animals as this black creature. Best avoid their presence. The old bison and his kind were one angle of a triangle of death. At one corner stood he and his kind, at the second the wild horse, at the third the Indian. All three were doomed. When the Spaniards brought their chargers to the New World, the Indians gained a splendid means to hunt the buffalo, which they formerly had been obliged to stalk on foot. First fate overtook the wild horse. Not much longer would it spare the bison. Last to fall would be the red man, dependent on the other two. And of all their fates the white man was the chief instrument.

The Morgan found no company in any of the living things abounding on the plains. Pronghorn antelopes, swift and shy, fled from him like the buffalo. Birds of the air—ducks, geese, quail, road runners—were solace only in that they lent life and movement to vast stillness. No more than that were the spry jack rabbits and the prairie dogs which sat up on their hindquarters and barked impudently from the edge of their holes at the wandering horse that once had come a cropper by stepping in one of those burrows.

The howling of coyotes broke the deathly quiet of the

long nights, but the Morgan hated their dismal yelping and their red-gleaming eyes dotting the encircling darkness. He recognized them for what they were—a gathering of hopeful, hungry ghouls, waiting for death or some crippling accident to overtake him. Their howling seemed more sinister to him even than the whirring of coiled rattlesnakes, which were only warning him not to tread on them.

For the horse, the prairie lost its charm and became harsh and stark. Poignantly he longed for green pastures, for the dark, warm safety of a stable. Just to be tethered to a wagon wheel would be enough. He found himself missing the feel of a halter or a bridle, even of a saddle on his back and the grip of a rider's legs on his barrel. How pleasant and reassuring a human voice would sound!

Not for the Morgan horse was the call of the wild. He had spent too long a time in man's service and companionship.

It was his longing for man that spurred him to travel steadily through and away from the Staked Plain toward distant, wooded hills. At length he reached and climbed up into them. Trees closed about him protectingly, and he lost the sense of utter solitude he had known in the prairie. Yet, his loneliness drove him onward, no less compellingly. Since none would seek him, he must seek.

But he *was* sought, or more exactly, awaited.

Yellow-green eyes were watching the solitary Morgan horse pushing steadily up the trail toward a mesa. They peered from the stout branch of a tree beside that trail. There, on not a few previous occasions, the mountain lion had successfully laid in wait for his prey.

The great, tawny beast was eight feet in length. He blended in with the leaves and their shadows cast by the sinking sun. This was early for him to hunt, but a ravenous hunger was gnawing fiercely at his belly. As he crouched on the limb, his long tail several times gently lashed his flanks, then froze into the rigidity of the rest of his body. His powerful muscles were gathered but not yet tense nor would they be until the instant they were needed.

Unsuspecting, the wind at his back, the Morgan horse climbed the trail. He would not journey much further but would bed down for the night on the mesa. He felt no premonition. Indians and black stallion were far behind him. In the hills he had encountered not even coyotes. There were no mountain lions, no cougars, in the experience of this horse from the East.

Had any human being watched him as he climbed toward that crouching death, pity, and an impulse to save him, would have filled the watcher's heart, stirred by man's hate for the beast of prey, and love for the beast of burden. Such a watcher would have been deaf to the words of the Psalmist: "The young lions roar after their prey, and seek their meat from God." But there was no human witness.

On came the black Morgan. When he was ten feet from the tree, the big cat, mad with hunger, could not prevent a twitching of his whiskers and the slightest tremor of the tip of his tail. Yet, with iron restraint, he let the horse approach closely and actually pass beneath the limb where he was poised.

At last, and very late, the horse caught that feral scent. With a desperate lunge, he sprang forward. But the mountain lion had pounced.

3: MASSACRE OF THE WAGONERS

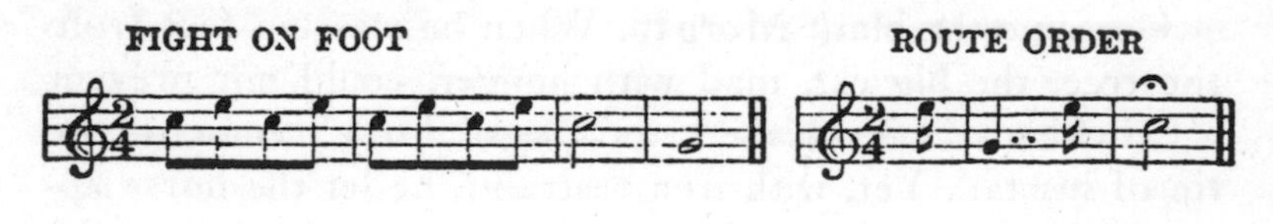

I

PETER SHANNON's father had been a captain of Union cavalry under Buford and Pleasanton in the Civil War. Growing up through that conflict, the youngster had desperately wished that every year would add two or three to his age so that he could ride off to war with his dashing sire. The best he had been able to manage was self-administered but intensive training in equitation and cavalry tactics on a fat and indignant pony.

Yet, his yearning and his effort had proved not altogether

in vain. When the high tide of the Confederacy had flowed north to Gettysburg, the home guard company of Peter's native town in Pennsylvania, mobilizing, had detailed him, only a lad of nine, as a despatch rider. After the war his father had taken him on long rides, the indolent pony replaced by a small, lively horse. Together, they had fought over the battles of the war, especially its cavalry engagements. The father had a veteran's heart's desire in his son: an eager and fascinated audience. And Peter in his father had a boy's heart's desire: an older man who forgot his age and treated him as a comrade—who made the pretended seem dramatically real and the past come alive.

"Remember this, Pete," his father would impressively declare. "Cavalry has to have mobility. That means it's got to be able to go places fast and be in shape when it gets there to fight or scout. There was a Reb general—corking good cavalryman by the name of Bedford Forrest—who said that the way to win battles was 'to get there fustest with the mostest men.' Good cavalry can do that. Now, what makes a cavalryman mobile?"

"His horse, sir," Peter answered promptly.

"Right. And that's why I've taught you to take care of your mount. What happens to you if he gets a saddle sore or goes lame from a stone inside a hoof you neglected to inspect?"

"Disciplinary action, sir," replied Peter. He wasn't quite sure what that was, but it didn't sound pleasant.

Together, they marched and maneuvered and charged an imaginary foe. John Shannon, enjoying it as much as the boy, taught him tactics as he once had his troop.

While the two breathed their horses after a gallop, the father would observe, "There's nothing like a smashing cavalry charge or a sweep around the enemy's flank. But get this into your head, my boy. Most of the time in the cavalry you turn over your mounts to the horse-holders, unsling your carbine and fight on foot. Sure, just like the infantry. And you make your fire power count. That's the lesson we Yank cavalrymen finally learned. After we learned that, Jeb Stuart and the rest of the Rebel cavalry didn't find it so easy to ride over us."

Once, they had ridden down to Gettysburg and retraced the ebb and flow of the tide of battle. Leading their horses through the great battlefield-cemetery, Peter remembered his father's deep voice reciting the last of President Lincoln's address.

" 'It is rather for us to be here dedicated to the great task remaining before us—that from these honored dead we take increased devotion to the cause for which they gave the last full measure of devotion; that we here highly resolve that these dead shall not have died in vain; that this nation, under God, shall have a new birth of freedom.' "

Over on the Little Round Top a bugler began sounding *Taps*.

"Stand to horse," Peter's father commanded quietly, and they remained at attention with heads bowed until the plaintively beautiful call had faded to a close. Peter would remember that, too, and the glisten of moisture in the corners of his father's eyes.

Now Peter was sixteen and ready for college. He wanted to go to West Point or enlist in the Army. "And whose fault is that?" his mother tartly had asked his father. The former captain of cavalry had laughed but ruled firmly against a martial career. There was, he declared, no future nowadays in the Army. Congress had cut it down to little more than a skeleton force, forgotten and neglected. Peter was scheduled to go to Yale, though not yet a while. Sixteen, his father insisted, was too young for college. Best hold the boy out for a year—not just to loaf but with something to do. Why not send him down to his Uncle Jim's ranch in Texas? He could ride and drive a team. He was handy with animals, and Jim, who had Government contracts for cattle and corn, would find him useful, not just a boarder.

Peter's gray eyes flashed. He ran a hand excitedly through his sandy hair. He had a warm, engaging grin and it lit up his face now. He did know and love horses, and riding the Texas range as a cowboy was an appealing prospect. It was the next thing to joining the cavalry.

"When do I leave, Pop?" Peter demanded.

But his mother strenuously objected. Texas, so far away, had been one of the Rebel States. Much of it was still wild, frontier country, and she had read of troubles there with the Indians. It was much too dangerous.

Peter's father replied that most of the Indian-fighting was in the West with the Sioux. William Tecumseh Sherman himself, General of the Army, had only recently stated that reports of Indian troubles in Texas were greatly exaggerated.

"Besides," he continued, speaking earnestly to his wife, "you must remember that Pete and I have lived through a great war from 1861 to 1865. It left its mark on both of us, though he was pretty young at the time. On me because I fought through it. On him because he wasn't old enough to. He needs the kind of active life he'll find in Texas to get it out of his system."

Peter nodded, his gray eyes serious. The Old Man could be a pretty understanding fellow sometimes.

Peter's mother sighed, then smiled and said: "Perhaps

you're right. Men are restless creatures, and ever since the war the two of you *have* been difficult."

II

Reins handled deftly, Peter Shannon guided his four-mule team. His wagon was the leading one in a train of ten hauling corn and other supplies from the railhead at Weatherford, Texas, to Fort Griffin. His Uncle Jim Long, the wagonmaster, rode on the seat at his side.

"Not sure I ought to have let you come along, young man," Jim Long remarked. "There's been all too many white men killed and scalped around here. Folks back East say it's safe. They don't know the Injuns in these parts."

He told Peter tales of the Kiowas and the Comanches. How the deadly Kiowas probably had killed more whites, man for man, than any other western tribe. How the even fiercer Comanches, the finest horsemen of the plains, had fought Spaniards and Mexicans for two centuries and still barred great areas of the Southwest to American settlement. Mighty bowmen were the Comanches—they could drive a shaft through a buffalo—and they were lancers unsurpassed by any of the crack cavalry regiments of Europe. But the Indians used those weapons only when they were short of ammunition for their modern repeating rifles, bartered with renegade traders for stolen horses.

"Those Injuns sure have helped fill the boot cemeteries—that's where men who died with their boots on get buried—and plenty of lonely graves along the trail," the wagonmaster continued. "There's one along here somewheres of a cowboy the Comanches caught. There. See yonder."

Peter leaned from his seat to read the epitaph crudely scrawled on a headboard:

"He was young and brave and fair,
But the Indians raised his hair."

"Don't mean to skeer you, young Peter," his uncle declared. "I'm just warning you, you've got to be on the lookout in this country. Reckon we're safe enough. There's Army posts here and there, and the soldiers patrol and do the best they can keeping the Injuns on reservations. If we should get jumped, you've got a rifle, and your Pa taught you how to shoot. Just keep on shooting, too. Don't give up ever. The Injuns don't believe in what we call the rules of civilized warfare. In case of an attack, remember the first thing to do, like I told you is—"

The wagonmaster started to his feet. He climbed up on the seat of the wagon and with all the strength of his lungs bawled:

"Corral!"

Peter, as he had been trained to do, swung his team off the road to the right, urging them into a trot. The other teamsters, shouting at their mules, closed up on him and followed as he doubled around. When Peter had closed the circle on the rear wagon, every teamster obeyed the wagonmaster's signal and turned his team sharply inward into the circle's center, pulled up and set his brakes. The wagon train was corraled. Wagoners jumped down to fill in the gaps between the white-covered "prairie schooners," building breastworks of sacks of grain.

That task would never be finished. The mass of Kiowas and Comanches, charging down on them, shooting as they came, gave no time.

III

In the wild confusion of that sudden onset Peter's mind was numbed. He knew that he dragged his rifle out of the leather boot fastened beside the wagon seat and emptied its magazine at the oncoming riders. He heard Uncle Jim's heavy Sharps banging. But amid the firing, the whooping and the shrill yipping, and the thunder of hooves, only one fantastic sound really penetrated his consciousness—the discordant blasts of a cavalry trumpet summoning the red horsemen to drive home their charge.

Two chiefs, gorgeous in warbonnets, charged into the circle. Each killed his man, counting coup, and rode through. After them a wave of horsemen surged against the corral. Still more Indians, dismounted, ran up and joined in the fray. A third and a fourth teamster went down under the fury of that first assault. Dimly seen through the smoke and dust, men fought hand-to-hand.

Then the Indians suddenly drew off and commenced galloping around the corral, yelping and pouring in a hot fire with Spencer carbines, breech-loading rifles, pistols, along with a hail of arrows.

From under the wagons, firing through wheels, the wagoners fought back. Red riders slipped from their ponies and were swallowed by the dust. But the fire from the corral was slackening. One dozen against one hundred and fifty. There could be only one result.

Peter heard his uncle's voice calling to him. It sounded hoarse and weak.

"Tell your mother—sorry I let you come. If they break in—again—run for the timber."

The voice fell silent. Peter, busy loading and firing his Winchester, did not realize that his uncle had died and that he was lucky to be dead rather than to have suffered a crippling wound. One of the charred bodies, later found in the wreckage of the wagon train, told the story. The teamster had been alive when the Indians chained him to a wagon wheel and lit a fire around him.

Skies were darkening. A big storm was gathering. In haste to finish, to kill and plunder, the circle of savage horsemen contracted and closed in. Again sounded the raucous trumpet blasts, like a hunting horn proclaiming the kill. Warriors leaped from their ponies and rushed the wagons. They streamed through the gaps, cut the mules loose from their harness, slit open corn sacks. The seven white men still on their feet made a break for the woods, two miles away.

Outside the shelter of the wagon corral and on the open prairie, Peter Shannon experienced a feeling of defenselessness that verged on sheer panic. He and the other six survivors were so few in the face of the scores of yelping braves now mounting up to gallop in pursuit. And the shelter of the woods seemed hopelessly distant.

"Fight on foot." His father's words kept echoing in his mind. "After we learned that lesson, the Rebels didn't find it as easy to ride over us."

Nor did the Indians. Furiously they charged down on the little knot of white men, only to break off the charge in the face of the fire of seven repeating rifles. But more joined in the assault. The teamsters, jumping to their feet and running toward the woods at every respite, gained less and less ground before they were forced to drop prone and start shooting again.

Peter was firing wildly. He knew it but could not help it. Each time the charge drove in closer.

British troops long wore their traditional scarlet uniform "for the terrible look of it"—because of the terror that fierce hue inspired in the foe. And here the flashing, savage color in the tide of these Indian charges struck similar dismay. Strips of red calico decked the streaming manes and tails of the galloping war ponies. The copper bodies of their riders were streaked and dotted vividly with war paint—vermilion torsos, blue owls on white-daubed chests, limbs striped with scarlet. On they came with yellow shields and couched lances and leveled carbines spurting crimson.

Peter saw a chieftain bearing down on him, glaring visage painted around the eyes with black lines which gave him the appearance of a sinister, half-human raccoon. The boy's hastily-fired shots missed the chief but brought down the rearing pony. Even in that desperate moment, Peter felt a twinge of pity for the horse.

Indian fire grew heavier, deadlier. The teamsters lacked any cover. In their next rush for the timber, two slumped to the ground and lay still. They were dead or as good as dead. Their comrades dared not stop.

Still, one long mile stretched interminably between them and the woods. Covering its bitter extent, grimly fighting off their pursuers, three more of the surviving five were hit. The wounded men struggled on.

Somehow they reached the edge of the woods. Gasping, they plunged in, each man for himself. None spared time to observe that their savage pursuers had turned back, no longer able to resist taking part in the looting of the wagons and the scalping and further mutilation of their fallen enemies.

Peter, unwounded but dazed and exhausted, stumbled on in among the trees. Their dark shadows began to envelop him. Gratefully he groped deeper. The deeper the harder for those yipping devils back there to find him.

The storm burst. Rain in torrents, rain that was almost a deluge, came flooding down.

4: THE TWAIN SHALL MEET

I

THE tree limb from which the mountain lion sprang was not high above the trail. For two reasons he had purposefully selected a lower branch. His pounce must be swift and sure, allowing his victim no time to lunge out from beneath. And with a large animal like a horse or a steer his method of slaughter was not to crush his prey to earth by his weight. Such a fall might break the slayer's grip and permit escape.

Even as it was, the sturdy legs of the black horse almost buckled under the impact of the great cat and the fearful shock of his attack. Square on the Morgan's back he lit.

The hooked claws of his forepaws fastened themselves in the horse's withers. Slavering jaws, surer than the stallion's, bit down through mane and champed till they met through quivering flesh. Hind claws dug in and clutched.

Two sounds rent the stillness of the gathering dusk and reverberated over the mesa. The Morgan's scream of mortal terror. The mountain lion's half-smothered roar of blood-lust, foreboding the kill.

Then commenced a ride of death.

To the mountain lion, it was not new. Often enough had he ridden it before, and always had it ended in the same satisfying climax: the rider feasting on his mount. For the black the experience was as strange as it was frightful. Yet, instinctively, he reacted just as must the first wild horse pounced upon by a cougar.

He bucked with all his might, bucked for his life. Thus, they say, American horses first learned how—with a mountain lion on their backs.

The Morgan, gentle of disposition, had never before done more than kick up his heels. Now he bucked and pitched like an unbroken mustang, like a chronic outlaw, kept for rodeos. One very brief pause had been sufficient to show him why he dare not stop bucking for an instant. The lion loosed the gripping claws of one hind leg, drew it forward and raked it bloodily backward across the ribs just above the belly. The black knew that if the enemy on his back were given half a chance, those cruel hind claws, powered by the mighty haunch muscles, would dig in deep and disembowel him.

He buck-jumped up the trail and out on to the mesa to give himself more room to shake off that dreadful incubus. He twisted and turned and swapped ends. But the big cat, growling and rumbling savagely in his throat, clung more tightly.

His stout heart, the endurance bred into him, carried the Morgan horse on. He bucked harder. Once he thought of trying to roll on the lion, but something made him aware that, once down, he was finished.

The lion's weight and his own strenuous exertions began to tell on him now. He was weakening, too, from loss of blood and the agony inflicted by teeth and claws. His feline foe, jolted and jarred though he was, sensed the approaching end. The rumbling in his throat softened almost into a purr.

II

To be lost in a dark woods at night under pouring rain is an unenviable experience, and the camping lore Peter Shannon's father had taught him served him little now. Except for his rifle, he lacked all the equipment on which he was accustomed to depend. Ax, poncho, food, frying pan—all were stowed in the wagons back on the prairie. An old hand would have improvised and made himself tolerably comfortable. The young fellow from the East was too utterly weary, still too apprehensive of pursuit, to do more than stumble ahead, a hand outstretched to keep him from colliding with trees.

It seemed impossible for it to rain so hard. Leafy branches were apparently no impediment to the drenching downpour. Soaked, miserable, Peter drove himself on. It came to the point where it took an effort of will to force one soggy, squelching boot ahead of the other.

Wet as he was, it seemed ridiculous for him to mind cold water running down his neck, but he did mind. Nor was this any time to start feeling hungry, he told himself. There was nothing he could do about it. Well, it just made more trouble to have your stomach clamoring.

Incessantly, in sheets, the rain flooded down. Peter repeatedly fell over tree roots. He took the falls on his right side, right hand outthrust into the clammy soil. Always he managed to remember that he must save his rifle and keep its muzzle from being clogged with mud.

All night he groped on, resting only a little now and then, leaning against a tree to listen for Indians who must surely be on his trail.

Through the beat of the rain and the whistling wind he could hear nothing; yet his imagination supplied all that his ears listened for vainly. Only when a cold, gray, still rainy day dawned did he find shelter of a sort under a fallen tree, partly upheld by branches, and sink into an exhausted and troubled sleep.

He woke, forced himself to his feet and pushed on. Without any idea of where he was going, he only knew that he could not stay where he was and starve.

Late in the afternoon he found some berries which were edible; at least they did not make him sick. He found also a stream, better for drinking than the muddy rain pools. The rain at last slackened and ceased. The trees were thinning now, and he was climbing. Perhaps before dusk he could reach a vantage point which would give him a view of the surrounding country.

The light began to fade. Peter had reconciled himself to another fear-haunted, lonely night when he unmistakably heard two such sounds as might have echoed through nightmares—a scream of terror and a blood-curdling roar.

III

"Get out of here quick! Don't be a fool," Peter told himself. But he seemed to be unable to take his own wise counsel. He levered one of his precious four remaining cartridges from his Winchester's magazine into the chamber and ran toward the sounds.

Snorts and throaty growls and pounding hooves guided him on to the mesa top where the Morgan horse was making his fight for life.

At first Peter saw only a black horse, bucking and pitching in such frenzied action as he had never witnessed. He watched, astounded. Then he caught sight of the rider clinging like a huge, yellow leech. He saw the mountain lion's head buried almost to the flattened, rounded ears in the mane of his victim, the tail switching, the fastened claws with blood streaming from their grip. He half raised his rifle, then lowered it. Never could he shoot the close-clinging beast without hitting the horse.

Peter's heart was torn with pity. Perhaps a shot in the air would scare the lion off. Again his brain warned him. A shot might well divert to him the fury of the lion, balked of his prey. And very likely it would draw the attention of any Indians in the vicinity.

Hesitant, he might have watched the drama to its end in helpless fascination. But the black horse had seen him. Here was man, long-sought through weary, lonesome days—man, his friend and protector—man who would save him in this moment of deadly peril.

The black galloped straight toward Peter.

An almost overwhelming impulse to turn and run back down into the woods seized upon the boy. An eight-foot mountain lion, blood-crazed with the imminence of a kill, was being carried toward him at full speed. No man could calmly await such an apparition. Only one who loved horses would have held his ground—and not many such.

But Peter had caught the frantic, beseeching look in the

Only one who loved horses would have held his ground

Morgan's wildly rolling eyes. He stood his ground, rifle ready.

The cougar, eyes and nose buried deep in mane, had not yet sensed the presence of a human on the scene. But he instantly was aware that the jolting buck-jumps had given way to a gallop. This was his chance. He drew up one hind leg for the fatal disemboweling stroke.

It was never delivered. A bullet, then another, thudded into his tawny body. Caution forgotten, Peter fired with the muzzle almost against the beast's hide. He loaded, and fired again until the magazine was empty. Snarling and screeching, the big cat relaxed his grip and slumped to the ground. On his back he clawed convulsively and spat at his enemy. Peter, shaking with rage and fear, clubbed his rifle and battered the flat skull until the malevolent yellow-green eyes glazed and the twitching body was still.

The boy straightened up unsteadily. He dropped his rifle barrel, stock splintered from it.

Night was falling. He moved toward the dark bulk of the black horse. Faltering, uncertainly, but irresistibly drawn, the horse moved toward him. This was his rescuer, company in his loneliness. Memories of a boy who once had fed him apples by the roadside came over him—a boy like this one.

The black horse stood quiet while his forehead was stroked. He pressed his muzzle against the friendly shoulder. When Peter twisted a hand in his mane near the poll and led him back toward the stream to bathe his wounds, the black horse followed gladly.

Between them passed the strong, heart-warming current felt when two meet, who all their lives will be fast friends.

5: RECRUITS FOR THE CROSSED SABRES

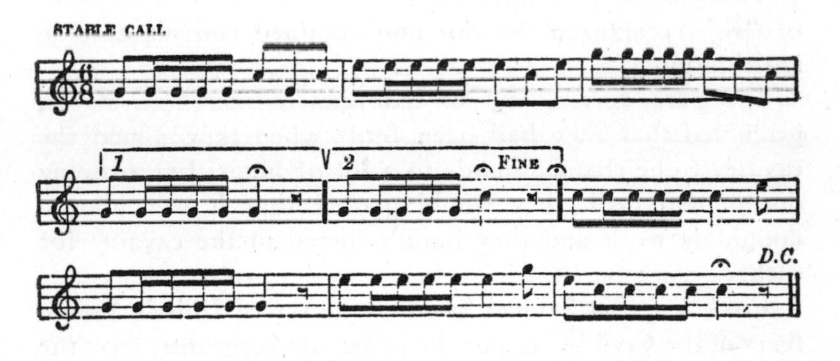

I

THE trumpeter of the guard sounded Stable Call. Its notes floated across the parade ground of the frontier Army post and set familiar words in the minds of listeners.

Come, get to the stable
As fast as you're able,
Water your horses and give 'em some corn.

For if you don't do it,
The Colonel will know it
And then you will rue it, as sure as you're born.

That summons produced its usual actions and reactions.

The trumpeter of the guard, an ex-lieutenant of Confederate cavalry named Elliot, told himself that the tone of his high G's was not all it should be, though as a matter of fact it was clear and bell-like.

Old Taylor, the guardhouse dog, a mournful mongrel with a strong bloodhound strain, gazed up at the trumpeter sadly in seeming agreement. High G's hurt his ears. He howled.

Private "Peruna" Simmons, the perennial prisoner, was marched out to perform post fatigue duties. Old Taylor, his confidant and companion, followed him.

Troop horses, from the bays of "A" Troop to the blacks of "K," recognized the call and stamped and nickered in anticipation.

Troopers, turning out of barracks to march to stable, grumbled that they had been fools when they joined the cavalry to be chambermaids to a lot of plugs. Later, doing dismounted drill, they would grouse that it was blasted doughboy work and they hadn't 'listed in the cavalry for such.

First Sergeant Samuel Smith, a major of Illinois Volunteers in the Civil War, and the other top sergeants, took the reports of platoon sergeants. From barrack walls echoed "— Platoon, present or accounted for" in an astonishing variety of accents. Yankee twangs and Southern drawls. The brogue of Sergeant Rourke, the guttural German of Sergeant Schmidt, and the rolled French R's of Sergeant Pinchon. Of such was the United States Army in the 1870's.

Captain Bone, Lieutenant Hatton, and all other troop

and platoon commanders, emerged from their quarters and strode toward the stables. In other regiments it might be possible to catch some extra sleep and let a junior officer or the sergeants take stables. But not in the 4th Cavalry. There you would "rue it, as sure as you're born."

In one set of the married quarters, Sally Ann Lindsay, fourteen, pushed back her chair from the breakfast table and announced that she was going to stand stables this morning. She would, her mother told her, do nothing of the sort —not after the language she had picked up there last time. Captain, Brevet Major Lindsay, arranged his adjutant's aiguilette, buckled on his sabre and hurried out to report to the Commanding Officer.

It was only six o'clock but Colonel, Brevet Major General Randall Slidell Mackenzie, commanding the 4th Cavalry, had taken his stand where he could scan the parade ground. If anything failed to happen that should happen or if anything happened that should not happen, those responsible would promptly discover the truth of the trumpet call's line: "The Colonel will know it."

But nothing untoward occurred. Horses were watered and fed and groomed carefully under the watchful supervision of troop officers and non-commissioned officers. A *click-click-click* sounded along the picket lines as brushes were knocked against currycombs to remove dust rubbed from sleek hides.

Yet, something unusual was taking place. At No. 2 Post the sentry had halted two early visitors—a boy and a black horse. The boy's clothes were tattered. He was haggard and limping. It seemed odd that he was not riding but only walking beside the horse whose mane he was clutching. Jagged, half-healed scars on the horse's back might be the explanation.

Peter Shannon was too weary to remember how he had found his way out of the hills—even how many days he and the horse had wandered. For the most part, he had wisely let the Morgan lead him. To that reliance, he was certain, he owed his life. Never once had the horse attempted to run away. He had seemed as desperately eager for Peter's companionship as the boy was for his, and the black was plainly grateful for Peter's care of the wounds. Footsore though he was, the boy never had tried to mount up on the scarred back.

Both of them had been on their last legs when they heard the trumpet call. As they reached the Army post to which it had guided them, both, the boy and the horse, experienced a strong sensation which was more than relief at finding human habitation. They seemed to have come to a place where they belonged.

But obviously that emotion was not shared by the corporal of the guard who had come at the sentry's call.

II

"Well, what's wanted, Number Two?"

Corporal Rick had just begun a quiet nap in the guardhouse and was annoyed at being disturbed. He was fairly tall and his uniform fitted well. His hair, deep auburn under the black campaign hat set at a jaunty angle, was a shade most women envied. A rakish type of good looks were undeniably his but they were marred by the sharp expression in his brown-green eyes and a habitual twist at the corners of his small mouth. He did not wait for an answer to his own question but snapped:

"A couple of tramps, eh? Trying to bum some handouts off the U.S. Army. Well, nothing doing. We don't eat none too well ourselves."

Peter started to speak but the other shut him off.

"Never mind the hard luck story. Heard it before. And if you're trying to sell the Army that nag—"

Peter, firing up, shouted at him: "I'd never sell this horse!"

"Not for much you won't," Rick retorted. "Move on, you and the crow-bait."

The sentry started to protest, "Aw, Corp," but desisted, knowing it would only earn him a tongue-lashing. Peter's pride would not let him make an appeal. He turned the Morgan and they moved off. Further along they might find a hospitable ranch.

"Hold on there," another voice called, its accent faintly Southern.

The trumpeter of the guard had walked up unobserved. Like Rick, he was tall and handsome, but debonair rather than swaggering. His hair was raven-black. In his dark eyes was a restless, searching look. Above the broad, point-down corporal's chevrons on his blue sleeves was the hunting horn insignia which indicated he was a trumpeter, an assignment also signified by two narrow, yellow stripes along his breeches, lighter blue than his blouse. Over his left shoulder was slung his brightly-polished trumpet.

"Hold on," he called again to the departing pair. "Rick, give the lad a chance. You never even took the trouble to question him."

"Mind your own business, Elliot," Rick snapped. "You're wearing no more stripes than me. I'm corporal of the guard and I know my duties."

"You are," the trumpeter conceded placatingly. "But both the boy there and the horse look like they've had a tough time. Reckon they might have information that'd interest

"The boy and horse look like they've had a tough time."

Headquarters?"

"Rats!" the other snarled. "Just tramps." The corners of his mouth took on a more sneering twist. He knew the trumpeter once had worn and still loved the Confederate gray—that, having been a Rebel officer, he was disqualified from holding a commission in the United States Army and must serve in the ranks. Rick was well aware how to irritate this man he both envied and disliked.

"You're due at the guardhouse, Corporal-Trumpeter," he said. " 'Little Boy Blue, go blow your horn.' "

Elliot flushed darkly. "Meet me back of the picket lines when we're off duty, Rick," he suggested, "and I'll drum a few more nursery rhymes into you." He turned his back on his opponent, went over to Peter and began questioning him rapidly and quietly. In a few moments he was facing the corporal of the guard again.

"Rick, this young fellow was one of the few that escaped from the wagon train massacre. The General will want to talk to him. You'd better notify the officer of the guard or I will."

Rick glared and swung away.

"Come along, young fellow. What's your name? Shannon? You look as if you could use some grub," Elliot said.

"My horse—" Peter began.

"I'll take care of him," the trumpeter assured him. "Think of your horse first, do you, young Shannon? I declare you'd make a right good cavalryman."

III

Fed, washed, his rags exchanged for fatigue clothes lent him by Elliot, Peter followed the officer of the guard to Headquarters. So he actually was to meet General Mackenzie of whom his father had talked so often. During the last months of the war John Shannon had served in the cavalry division commanded by the General. Mackenzie's dashing leadership and striking personality had made him his troop commander's hero. Peter could picture his father's eyes shining now and hear him holding forth on General "Mac."

"Graduated Number One in his class at West Point, my boy. That takes doing. In the war he won four brevets for gallantry and was wounded I don't know how often. At Second Bull Run he was shot through the shoulders. Soon as he could sit up he wrote his mother: 'I am wounded in the back but I was not running away.' At Petersburg he was right up in the line directing fire, and two fingers of the hand he was pointing with were shot off. He led a charge at Winchester down on the Reb batteries, carrying his hat up on the point of his sabre. Shell cut his horse in two. General Mac looked up from the ground where he was binding his bleeding leg with a handkerchief and said, 'That's what you call dismounting without the numbers.'

"I tell you, Peter, the man was incredible. He was hit in the foot and then in the leg at Cedar Creek. One horse was killed under him. A round shot bowled him off his second mount and stunned him. When he came to, he couldn't use his arms—temporarily paralyzed. He ordered himself lifted back into the saddle and resumed command.

"Believe me, you soldiered under General Mac. Everybody was scared not to. He was a strict disciplinarian, like his father before him. His father, who was a commander in the Navy, hanged three men for mutiny on his brig and one of 'em was the son of the Secretary of War. Some of the men General Mac disciplined vowed they'd shoot him in the back during the next battle. Then they'd see him out in front leading a charge and they'd cheer their lungs out for him and follow anywhere he led. You've got to have discipline. Without it an army's just a mob. And what's a youngster without discipline, Pete?"

"A brat, sir," Peter had answered, grinning.

"Right. There's a long chance you might run into Mackenzie. He's stationed somewhere in Texas, where you're going. If you do, he won't remember me but present my respects."

Peter straightened his shoulders. Now he was being ushered into the presence of his father's hero.

The two stars of Mackenzie's brevet rank gleamed on his shoulder straps but glowed no brighter than his eyes, which seemed to burn into you. In the cast of his countenance was some of the dourness of his Scotch forebears. The habit of command had compressed his mouth under its dragoon's mustache, and there were lines graven by pain from old wounds and rheumatism. Yet, strong in him was a sense of loyalty, of justice and of generosity. Evidence of those traits often lightened the stern look he usually wore.

Peter stood at attention in front of the General's desk and said as his father had taught him: "Sir, Peter Shannon reports to the Commanding Officer."

Mackenzie smiled. "You've been in the Army? No, you're too young."

"My father was, though, sir. A captain of cavalry. He served under the General at Five Forks and Appomattox and told me to present his respects."

Mackenzie knit his brow for an instant and said: "Yes, John Shannon. I remember him well. A very able officer. One of my best troop commanders."

Warm with pride at the praise of his father, Peter was able to give a graphic account of the massacre of the wagoners, though the memory of it still sent shivers up and down his spine. The General put many questions. He must find and punish the guilty Indians. The 4th Cavalry had not reached the scene until the next morning when all tracks had been washed out by the heavy rain.

Finally the General declared: "Your uncle's dead and you are lucky to be alive. I'll see to sending you back home to your family."

"Please, sir, I don't want to go," Peter protested. "I'd like to join the Regiment and serve against the Indians that killed Uncle Jim."

"You're too young," Mackenzie ruled, "though I might enlist you as a trumpeter. But not without your parents' consent."

"I think they'll consent now, sir. I'll write at once."

"Very well. Meanwhile, I'll attach you for rations as a civilian employee. You might be able to help us spot some of those raiders, if they're back on the reservation."

"Thanks a lot, sir. I'll do all I can. But there's one more thing. There's my horse—the one I found and brought in—or he brought me in."

"If you join up, young Shannon, you'll have to dispose of him. Only officers are entitled to private mounts. Maybe you could ship him home."

"We'd kind of like to stick together, sir."

Mackenzie's dour look softened. "I understand. Well, I tell you, Shannon, if he's sound, you can sell him to the Government, and I'll assign him to your troop. What is he? A black? To 'K' Troop then." The General smiled. "I'm talking as if you both were already in the 4th."

So they were—in Peter's imagination. As in a rosy dream coming true, he saw himself in Army blue, the crossed sabres of the cavalry on his jaunty forage cap, yellow stripes down his breeches. He was astride the Morgan horse. Indian bullets were whistling by, and the black curveted and pranced a little but in defiance, not fear. Peter controlled him easily, reins in his left hand, trumpet at the carry in his right. The entire 4th Cavalry in column of squadrons, sabres drawn, rose in stirrups as General Mackenzie turned and commanded: "Trumpeter, sound the charge!"

Nobody could daydream with impunity in Mackenzie's presence. What the general actually said, breaking through Peter's martial imaginings, was a gruff "That's all."

Peter jumped and took a hasty departure.

6: MOUNT AND TROOPER

I

AFTER several weeks on the sicklist to recover from his wounds, the black Morgan was examined and passed as sound by the veterinary and duly bought as a remount by the United States Government. He was neatly shod by a blacksmith. Then he was turned into the corral of "K," the black horse troop.

He merged into what might be called a miniature Black Sea, where tossing heads, waving tails and constantly-shifting, glossy bodies produced the effect of waves rolling over an expanse of dark ocean. Adjoining corrals of other troops —not all twelve troops of the 4th Cavalry were now stationed at the post—showed other color separations. There were two troops of bays, dark and light; two of sorrels; one of chestnuts; and one of grays, including a number of white horses, called grays in the Army. The mounted band and the regimental trumpeters also rode grays, in conformance with an ancient custom for cavalry musicians.

This system of color separation improved the appearance of an outfit and aided in its identification at a distance; also it made easier the cutting out of horses, mixed in a herd. Only in one case was the color scheme ruined. Luckless Headquarters Troop had been forced to take all the leftovers and odd shades. In consequence, it was a hodgepodge of roans, piebalds or pintos, buckskins, and claybanks which, being duns with black-striped legs, a black streak down their backs, and black manes and tails, reminded one somewhat of zebras. They were all good horses, but Headquarters Troop suffered from a sense of inferiority and a nickname of "The Brindles."

The descendant of Justin Morgan had joined a crack troop when he was loosed among those horses all of his own color. The members of "K," mounted on their black steeds, considered themselves, as black horse troops often do, altogether the most dashing and formidable outfit in the Regiment. And the horses carried themselves as if they completely concurred.

But the newcomer was at once shown that, although his hide was the right hue, he did not yet belong. It was exactly like a new boy arriving for his first day at school. The old horses trotted up to look him over critically and sceptically. Some of them, like members of the student council appointed to welcome freshmen, cordially rubbed noses with him. Others, holding aloof until this ceremony was over, pranced over with obvious intent. This new fellow had best be put in his place, and there was no time like the present to do it. A little hazing was in order.

One of them bit at the Morgan's ears. Another aimed a kick at his ribs. A third charged down on him, scuffling up dust. Other troop horses stood around to watch the fun.

The Morgan had run for his life from the black stallion on the *Llano Estacado*. But he was taking nothing from such as these. Snorting and squealing, he whirled on his attackers. More agile than they, he avoided most of their kicks and bites. In the first few minutes he managed three sharp nips in return and landed with a resounding whack of hooves on one opponent. Twice, he dodged the horse that liked to charge. The third time he countered with a charge of his own. He plunged into the other, took him off balance, hit him hard with a sturdy shoulder and bowled him over, rolling him in the dust.

The jamboree ended only when the stable guard came shouting into the corral and broke it up. The Morgan had proved himself and was accepted. Only the equine bully, who had done the charging, showed a disposition to quarrel on. He was quelled by a heavy black named Big Bill, who was the First Sergeant's horse and lived up to it by acting as one having authority. At times he relaxed and played the clown. Big Bill had been taught tricks in his younger days. To the immense discomfiture of his dignified rider, he would sometimes sit down on his haunches, like a dog or a cat, to rest.

Some of the other sergeants' mounts—Old Lead, Birdshy, and the mare Suzette—made friends with the new black.

All the goings-on in the corral had been watched from a

corner of the fence with interest and amusement by Major Lindsay, the Adjutant, an experienced and devoted horseman. He had enjoyed the little drama of the Morgan's arrival. Now, as the dust settled, he scrutinized the new horse more closely.

First-rate cavalry mount, he adjudged. Must be the animal brought in by the young fellow who got away from that wagon train massacre. Morgan horse by the look of him. Doubt if there's even been a cross there. Wouldn't mind owning that little black myself. Reminds me of General Sherman's Rienzi—a three- or four-year-old Morgan gelding, too, when I knew him in the War. Coal black and white feet like this one. But Rienzi's taller—about sixteen hands.

Through Major Lindsay's head ran some lines of the stirring poem on Sheridan's ride to rally Union troops routed at Cedar Creek. Thomas Buchanan Read had written it only a few days after the battle.

"Be it said, in letters both bold and bright:
'Here is the steed that saved the day
By carrying Sheridan into the fight,
From Winchester—twenty miles away!' "

Fine cavalryman, Phil Sheridan, the Major mused. Commands the Department of the West, and we'll be seeing him down here one of these days. His name is recorded in history as one of our best generals in the War of the Rebellion. Yet, I'll bet that seventy or eighty years from now a good many people will remember his name chiefly from that poem—about him and his horse.

And this black Morgan here in the corral is the spit and image of Rienzi, except for size, right down to the white feet. Let me think, though. Rienzi had three white stockings. This fellow has four. Yes, four. *Cuatralbo,* as the Mexcans say.

Why, I've seen this horse before! I'll swear that's the black Morgan I bargained for with that Vermonter when I was out buying remounts. Old Tafoya, the *Comanchero,* got him. This youngster who's joining up as a trumpeter brought that horse in. Must have stolen him from Tafoya. Not that I care what's rustled off that old buzzard, but he probably can prove ownership in this case, and there's bound to be trouble if he spots this horse, bought and branded "U.S." That young recruit isn't as innocent as he looks.

"Farrier," the Major shouted.

A soldier emerged from the stable. "Yes, sir, Major," he answered.

"Find that recruit who just came into your troop and have him report to me at my quarters at once."

II

Peter Shannon still found it hard to realize that he was actually enlisted in the United States Cavalry. He could guess at the arguments his father had used to persuade his mother. Concentration on school would have been difficult after what had happened to Uncle Jim—after all he had gone through himself. "Get it out of your system," John Shannon had written. "I'll give you a year or two. Then I'm buying you out and sending you off to college. And no argument." There had been an added proviso that he work in some studying.

Peter's present errand, however, convinced him that he had undoubtedly joined up. He had been ordered to draw uniform and equipment at the quartermaster warehouse and was now engaged in signing for a miscellany of articles worth more money than he ever had had or ever hoped to have.

Across the counter Quartermaster Sergeant Connors, gray and wizened, confronted him with the suspicious air habitual to quartermaster sergeants, bank tellers, and the like. But there was a twinkle in his one remaining eye. The other had been lost in battle, in the Civil War, said Sergeant Connors, but in reality it was in the Mexican War at Buena Vista.

"By the name iv yez, Recruit Shannon, there's Irish blood in ye," observed the old veteran. " 'Tis gin'rally acknowledged that the Irish are the bist soldiers in the U.S. Army. Such bein' the case, I'll not be issuin' yez the ould and worn equipment I was plannin' to git off me shelves but only the bist iv iv'rything."

"Thank you, sir," Peter responded politely.

"Nivver say 'sor' to a non-commissioned officer," the other corrected. "Now watch what I give yez and what ye'll be owin' Uncle Sam for."

Peter stared in utmost fascination while arms, clothing, and equipment were heaped before him. In a practiced singsong, interspersed with illuminating asides, Sergeant Connors enumerated:

"Wan carbine, Springfield, Model iv 1869, breech-loader, single-shot, calibre .45. (And a foine little wan-shot gun it is, though officers and min who kin buy Henry and Remington rep'atin' rifles does so, and the hos-tile Injuns does likewise from rapscallion traders, bliss thim.)

"Wan sling, carbine. . . . Wan revolver, Colt, Army Model, calibre .44 complate with holster. (Six shots—six Injuns, if aimed with care and fired whin too clos't to the varmints for comfort.) Wan sabre, scabbard, and belt. (Ye could stick the inemy quicker and further away with the ould lance.) Wan trumpet, with yellow worsted to be braided for sling. The deadliest weepon iv thim all, Recruit Shannon, and nivver let me catch yez practicin' on it anywheres in me hearin'."

The heaps on the counter grew higher and broader. The excellent saddle invented by General McClellan, and numerous other horse equipment: saddle blanket, nose-bag, heavy leather halter, iron picket pin with long lariat, two horseshoes with extra nails, currycomb, horsebrush, and more; personal equipment such as a pair of gray woolen blankets, canteen, haversack, tin coffee cup. Peter passed from a state of fascination to one of dismay.

"With all that stuff on me and on my horse, how'll I ever get into the saddle, Sergeant?" worried Peter begged.

"We hoist yez aboard with a derrick, me boy," Connors declared. "There ye sit, fortified before and foreninst by goods and accourtymints. Jist don't ivver git off and ixpict to git on agin unless the derrick's handy."

Peter, in the usual hazy and confused state of a recruit, was uncertain whether to believe the derrick yarn or laugh.

Items of uniform followed. Stable frock of white cotton. Boots and spurs. Campaign hat and forage cap. Jacket of dark blue and breeches of lighter blue, with reinforced seat, an advantage pointed out by Sergeant Connors with a grin and the remark:

"Ye'll be glad iv that. 'Twas said iv the First Iowa after hard service in the late war that they nivver would run from the inemy nor a lady. And why not? yez ask. Sure and they had no sates in their britches."

The Sergeant shoved over the uniform with additional advice. "Have thim clothes altered to fit yez by your company tailor. He'll be the soldier ye see tryin' to mount his horse from the off side.

"And by the by, ye'll sign for your horse, too. Nivver be forgettin' that if he or any iv the rist iv this stuff is missin' not in line of duty, Private Shannon, P., pays for it. Whin yez draw jist sixteen dollars a month, figure out some toime how long it'll take yez to settle for a lost horse prancin' acrosst the pay roll to the chune iv $132.50."

With which sage counsel, Quartermaster Sergeant Connors waved him away. Peter had picked up the first load to carry to barracks when an orderly called from the doorway.

"Shannon there? All right. Report to Major Lindsay at his quarters. You better make it on the double, Rookie."

III

Peter, hurrying up to the Adjutant's quarters, was confronted by a girl leaning on the gate of the picket fence inclosing the small yard. His glance was brief and casual, but big, hazel eyes, a saucy nose with freckles on it, and glossy, brown hair braided into two, fat pigtails registered on his consciousness. She did not move but smiled up at him. Her teeth were small and very white.

"Hello, boy," she greeted him.

Boy! The nerve of her! In spite of long, thin legs like a colt's, she couldn't be more than twelve. Well, give her fourteen at the most. "Boy" from her—and to a Regular cavalryman. Of course, Peter had not yet had a chance to get into his uniform, but the snip ought to be able to see. He'd put her in her place. He'd fix her.

"Hello yourself, brat," he snapped back contemptuously.

She didn't seem to mind in the least. Peter was surprised into asking why she didn't object to being called a brat.

"I *am* a brat, an Army brat," she avowed. "All Army

children are called brats and I guess we really are—sort of." She smiled again, and Peter could not help noticing that when she did, her nose wrinkled a little and became even saucier. "Mother says I've never been taken in hand enough. When I was younger, Mother was sick quite a bit, and most of the time the only nurse I had was a soldier—Pop's dog-robber."

"Dog-robber?"

"My father's striker—his soldier orderly. You *are* ignorant, aren't you?" She flashed that impish, impudent smile at him again.

"I—"

"Lots of the time I was tethered to the post flagpole with a lariat or picketed just like a horse to keep me from straying. But I broke loose. I never did care for hanging around quarters. I like it down at the stables or at the mule skinners' lines, but Mother says I pick up bad language there."

Peter, who was unable to resist laughing, now tried again to break in, but vainly. The girl was wound up.

"Pop is going to give me a derringer," she announced. "He says I'm old enough now to carry one and use it in an emergency. Mother's had one for years. Once when Pop and a small escort were bringing her and me in an Army ambulance through bad Indian country—"

Peter succeeded in stemming the flow. "Listen, what's-your-name," he interrupted. "I've—"

"Sally Ann," the girl supplied. "Just let me tell you this first. This is what Pop told Mother then. He said, 'If the Indians jump us, and I'm hit, you'll know what to do. You've got your derringer. Remember the squaws are crueler than the bucks. *Don't let 'em get the baby or you alive!* And that's really true, boy. If *you* knew Indians—"

Peter's outburst was indignant enough to gain him the

floor. "I kind of think I do!" he flared. "A while ago I was a teamster in a wagon train that—"

"Oh!" cried Sally Ann. "Were *you* in *that?* Tell me *all* about it."

She proved to be a good listener and a flattering one. Peter began to admit to himself that she was rather likable, after all. He went on to tell her about himself—how he had enlisted and was to be a trumpeter in Troop "K."

"The best d— darn troop in the whole d— pardon me—in the whole regiment," Sally Ann enthusiastically acclaimed. The girl spied yellow worsted strands protruding from one of Peter's pockets.

"That's for your trumpet sling," she identified it, pointing. "Let me braid it for you. You probably don't know how, and goodness knows I've had practice enough on these pigtails."

Sally Ann braided while Peter held ends. Such was the tableau beheld by Major Lindsay when he stepped out on his porch. Abruptly, Peter snapped to attention, saluted and said:

"Sir, Private Shannon, 'K' Troop, reports to the Adjutant as ordered."

"My orders were: report at once. That was a good half-hour ago. Is there any reason for the delay?" demanded the officer coldly.

"Well—no, sir, none," Peter answered.

"The deuce there isn't!" Sally Ann exclaimed. "Pop, I was the delay."

"That doesn't justify it in the least," her father ruled sternly.

"Oh, come on, Pop. He's only a rookie," Sally Ann pleaded.

Peter drew himself up even straighter. Angrily and loftily he addressed the girl.

"I may be only a recruit," he declaimed, "but I am the son of a soldier who taught me—or tried to teach me—obedience to orders." Peter faced toward her father and repeated: "Sir, I have no excuse."

Major Lindsay shooed the suppressed and discomfited Sally Ann indoors.

"Now, Shannon," he said, "I've heard the story you told the General about that horse you brought into the post and sold to the Government. I will not at this time question your assertion that you found him out on the range. Let it stand that the horse was strayed, not stolen. But I happen to remember that black Morgan well and I know his owner. The horse must be returned to him immediately."

Peter relaxed from his rigid attention. He stretched out one hand in an imploring gesture, and his mouth worked in mute protest, though he spoke no word. What good would any word do? The horse he had saved, the horse that had led him out of the wilderness, was beyond his control now, sold to the Government, and inevitably to be returned to his rightful owner.

7: A QUESTION OF OWNERSHIP

I

No REPORT of the raid by Southern Cheyennes which gave the black Morgan his freedom ever had reached Headquarters of the 4th Cavalry. Such affairs were commonplace in the Texas Panhandle. Army garrisons, few and widely scattered, were far too occupied to concern themselves with the killing of a few men by Indians, particularly if the victims were Mexicans, or with the running off of a horse herd or other plundering. If Mackenzie had had word, he would undoubtedly have remarked: "So the Cheyennes knocked off old José Pieda Tafoya, did they? Good for them. Saves me trouble. I always meant to hang the old devil first chance I got."

But the Indians on the reservations knew of the raid. The Comanches and the Kiowas were angry at the Cheyennes for trespassing on their territory and for cutting off such a useful source of arms and firewater as Tafoya. They were forced to deal with other *Comancheros*—Caddo Jim, a Caddo Indian, and the like—and these boosted their barter rates. However, the Indians naturally told nothing of the story of *Señor* Tafoya's bad luck. Let soldiers continue to believe that Tafoya was alive and active. It would divert their attention from other arms traders.

Major Lindsay, reporting his positive knowledge of the ownership of the Morgan horse to General Mackenzie, emphasized the embarrassment to the Army which a claim by the rightful owner would cause.

"You're right, Lindsay," the Commanding Officer concurred. "If I ever catch Tafoya, and have the scrap more evidence against him I need, he must have no countercharge that might save his neck. He must not be able to say the U.S. Army stole a horse of his. Where is the old scoundrel now?"

"We don't know, sir. Haven't heard of him for some time. He must be lying low."

"And up to something," Mackenzie added. "But don't hold on to the idea that young Shannon rustled the horse. His father served under me in the War, and I'll vouch for the boy."

"Very well, sir. What disposition will be made of the horse?"

"Return him—without my compliments—to Tafoya, but

make no special effort to find the man. That bad penny will turn up. Meanwhile . . . well, keep quiet about the whole business and let the horse do troop duty. He might get killed in our next Indian fight. I'd say that would be better for him than being turned back to José Pieda Tafoya."

The Adjutant nodded grimly. "It certainly would, sir, from all I've heard of the way Tafoya treats horses."

II

The Morgan horse neighed and trotted up to the corral fence when he sighted his master. It was almost more than Peter could bear. No matter how prized, how loved a possession, it becomes more precious still when about to be lost.

Peter gulped back a lump in his throat. He entered the corral and flung an arm around the arched neck, rubbing the hollow between the bones of the lower jaw and laying his face against the velvet muzzle. The horse snorted softly and wrinkled his nose affectionately against the boy's cheek.

Peter thought: They're going to take him away from me, and I don't even know his name.

So this was a Morgan horse. That was what Major Lindsay had said, and now Peter recognized characteristics he had failed to notice. His father had talked a good deal about Morgans, his regiment having once been brigaded with the 1st Vermont Cavalry.

"It was one of the finest marching and fighting regiments in the War," John Shannon had told him, "and a lot of the credit for that was due to its mounts being almost all Morgans. At Gettysburg it charged five Rebel infantry regiments and two batteries. I remember a line from the final report of the colonel of the Vermonters: 'Were charging enemy when order came to stop fighting.'

"Grand horses, Morgans," Peter's father mused. "Since this nation was young, they've hauled logs, stone boats, plows and barges. They've won races. Taken the doctor to his patients, families to church. We've fought our wars from their backs. They're helping to win the West now.

"And they're all of the great line founded by a little bay stallion. Some say he was sired by the blooded steed of a Tory colonel, stolen when he was tied outside a tavern, by three American soldiers in our Revolution. Whatever his blood, Justin Morgan must have been a remarkable horse to leave the descendants he has."

Peter stroked the black's small, wide-set ears. He said to himself: "I'll call my horse that—Justin. After his forefather. Justin . . . it's a good name. Isn't it, old fellow?" He stood back at an arm's length and regarded the black. The horse gazed back at him out of dark, expressive eyes and tossed his head.

"Justin it is then," Peter decided. Half-aloud he told himself: "Dad always wanted a Morgan but never did get one. Now here I have one of my own." He loved this horse more than he had his first pony—more than the horse he'd left at home. They'd been through so much together.

Suddenly, he emerged from his daydream and remembered. He didn't own the Morgan. Someone else did, and the Army was going to give him back to that owner as soon as he could be found.

Peter turned abruptly and hurried out of the corral. He could not quite wink away the moisture in his eyes. The sun glistened on it and betrayed him to Corporal Rick who was walking by. That auburn-haired trooper planted himself in Peter's path, arms akimbo on his hips, a sneer curling the corners of his small mouth.

" 'Weep no more, my lady,' " he sang, tauntingly.

Crimson with mortification and rage, Peter glared at him, fists clenching. For a few moments he was unable to speak. Then some advice of his father's came back to him: "Don't ever lose your temper, son, if you can help it, even if you're about to get into a scrap. You'll put up a better fight if you've got some sort of control over yourself."

So he managed to speak in fairly even tones. "You've got stripes on your sleeves, Corporal. Maybe I'm only a rookie but I know the regs. about striking a non-com. Now if you—"

"—if I took off my shirt with the chevrons on it?" "Hay" Rick finished for him. "Why, certainly. Happy to oblige. Always do anyways before I spank children."

He was unbuttoning his shirt when a soft Southern voice sounded behind him. "Reckon you forgot, Hay, you had a previous engagement with me down by the picket line," reminded Corporal-Trumpeter Elliot.

"Little Boy Blue again," Rick drawled. "I'll get around to you soon as I've slapped some discipline into this infant."

"No, Hay," Elliot answered, stepping in front of him. "I can't wait. I'm one of these fiery, headstrong Southerners you hear about."

"The kind we just got done licking the daylights out of?"

"Yes, that kind. But I don't seem to remember it so well. Now if you would be kind enough to refresh my memory, Corporal—"

"Happy to oblige, Corporal. Come on—"

Peter pushed in between the two, both a head taller than he. Hands against chests, he shoved them back.

"What's the matter with you two?" he yelled furiously. "It's *my* fight!"

"Nobody's fight."

Tall First Sergeant Smith was standing over them. He looked stern but there was a trace of a grin on his bearded face. "Nobody's fight, bantam," he told Peter. "Not yours, not anybody's. Elliot, Rick, get back to quarters. There'll be no fighting in this troop. Save it for the Indians."

III

Every boy, every young man, should have an older man—or several—to whom he can look up. A man or men he trusts and respects and admires almost to the point of worship. Someone he can follow and pattern himself after and count upon in time of trouble. This idol may or may not be his father. If it fails to be, that is one of the quiet tragedies of life.

Peter's father measured up and held his place in the boy's heart. But he was far away. Fortunately, there were others to supplement him, and John Shannon himself would have been glad that it was so, for he wisely knew his son's need. And these older men of his son's choice were men his father would have chosen for him.

It was not Mackenzie. To Peter he was one to be followed loyally, to be greatly respected, too, but he was remote and regarded with awe not unmixed with dread—a Jehovah of the Thunders. Nor was it Captain Bone or Lieutenant Hatton of Troop "K," fine officers and likable personalities though they were. On his pedestals Peter placed First Sergeant Samuel Smith, the ex-major of Volunteers, and Corporal-Trumpeter Lance Elliot, the former captain of Confederate cavalry.

Sergeant Smith, big—six feet four inches tall—and bearded, was a martial figure, yet the look of a scholar clung to him. Indeed, he had been a college professor, a fine and inspiring teacher. Four bloody years in the Civil War had finished that career for him. Too restless to return to quiet civilian pursuits, like many another veteran, he had followed the only alternative he found possible: reenlistment in the Army. In spite of his excellent record as a squadron commander, he could obtain no commission. Congress had drastically reduced the Army, and there were many applicants for every vacancy. In the 4th Cavalry every officer above the rank of second lieutenant was a Civil War veteran; the "shavetails" generally were young West Pointers.

As the Top Sergeant was a man out of his rightful niche, so was Corporal Elliot a man out of his time. The son of a wealthy planter, he had belonged to the chivalry of the Old South where medieval knighthood had flowered again briefly, only to fade forever. Young Elliot had fought two duels. Wearing as a favor the scarf of his lady fair, he had mounted steed, couched lance and ridden in ring tilts. Rather than dispel the dream, the War had caused it to glow brighter. Elliot had ridden singing into battle, sabre flashing, a captain on the staff of that dashing cavalier, J. E. B. Stuart. With peace had come his family's ruin and a disillusionment with life so bitter it was almost desperate. It put him into a Yankee uniform, making a mere trumpeter of him. But at least he still had a horse between his legs and a sword at his side. And if the Comanches were no red knights so far as obedience to the precepts of chivalry was concerned, they were among the finest horsemen in the world and not unworthy foemen.

Where these two—Smith and Elliot—led, young Peter Shannon followed. They taught him the lore of that gallant arm, the cavalry, and told him tales of the old Dragoons who once had held these same Texan marches against the Indians.

Elliot sang the *Dragoon Song* for Peter, accompanying himself on the banjo which Joe Sweeny, Jeb Stuart's banjo player, had taught him to strum.

Oh! the dragoon bold he knows no care,
As he rides along with his uncropped hair;
He spends no thought on the evil star
That sends him away to the border war.

His form in the saddle he lightly throws
And on the moonlight scout he goes,
And merrily trolls some old time song
As over the trail he bounds along.

Oh, blithe is the life a soldier leads
When a lawless freedom marks his deeds,
And gay his path o'er the wildwood sod
Where a white man's foot hath never trod.

Then cheer, boys, cheer for the girls afar.
We'll all go home at the close of the war,
And sadly tanned by a Southern sun,
We'll spin long yarns of the deeds we've done.

His mentors taught Peter pride in his own regiment. The 1st Dragoons had become the 1st Cavalry ("once commanded by Robert E. Lee," Elliot informed him, his eyes shining) and in 1861 the 1st had furnished *cadre* to form the 4th, which had made a valiant record throughout the Civil War, participating in seventy-six actions—gallant charges to long, sweeping raids.

But Peter could never banish the worry that kept gnawing at him. He had his heart's desire in being a cavalryman, yet a cavalryman was not a cavalryman without a mount, and he stood to lose his at any moment. Of course, they would assign him some nag or other when his present horse was returned to his owner. But his devotion and dependence belonged to the black Morgan, Justin. Without him even a career under the crossed sabres of the cavalry seemed without savor. Never, with Justin gone, could he, like the dragoon bold, ride away to the border war and "know no care."

IV

Sally Ann Lindsay found Peter at the corral where he spent much of his off-duty time with the horse he expected to see so little longer. She surveyed him critically and completely, from head to foot—the forage cap cocked a little to the right, the trim cavalry jacket, blue breeches stuffed into black boots, spurs glinting at their heels. Her big, brown eyes lit with frank approbation.

"Hi, soldier," she greeted him.

Peter grinned. "Promoted me, haven't you? It was 'boy' last time."

The girl gave him an answering smile. "Listen," she began a bit breathlessly. "I'm not supposed to be down here. I've been ordered to keep away from stables. If I'm caught, somebody will take a pair of issue hairbrushes and beat the long roll on my little—. Excuse me but I forget to be ladylike."

Sally Ann blushed a little under the freckles, then hurried on. "The other day I butted in when you were reporting and you got kind of mad at me and I can't say I blame you."

"Aw, that's all right. Forget it." Peter was a little embarrassed. When the girl looked at him appealingly like that, he felt sort of stirred up inside.

"So I found out what all the shooting was about," she bubbled on. "I pumped Pop—and maybe I don't know how!

'He is no more than clay in my fair hands.' (That's something I read in a novel.) Well, the fuss was about your mount, wasn't it? And I bet it's this black gelding with four white feet right here."

Justin, head over the top rail, had been gazing at the pair throughout the conversation, with no attention whatever paid to him. He looked a little miffed.

At Peter's nod of confirmation, Sally Ann flung her arms around the black's head. "Oh," she exclaimed, "isn't he a *darling!* No wonder you feel about him the way you do."

A little jealously Peter watched the love scene between Sally Ann and Justin, but his heart felt warm and his eyes were a little misty.

"Know who he belonged to?" the girl cried, jerking her face out of the horse's thick mane. "A dirty old *Comanchero* named José Pieda Tafoya. He sells guns to the Indians to kill our troops and gets 'em liquored up on squirrel whiskey."

"Squirrel whiskey?"

"Sure. Makes 'em want to go out and climb a tree. Red lightning. Rotgut stuff. Well, sir, some Cheyennes caught Tafoya, the old buzzard, t'other day—caught him dead to rights. So cheer up, Private Shannon. Looks like you'll stay mounted. The Cheyennes sculped old Tafoya proper."

"Scalped him!"

"You bet. Pop just got the story from Caddo Jim, another Indian trader. It sounds straight. Caddo Jim wouldn't have any reason to lie."

In his joy, Peter grasped both the girl's hands in his. Then he flushed and dropped them hastily.

Said Sally Ann, her cheeks a little red, too: "Drop in at our kitchen some aft. Ma Simmons, she's our cook and a spike at 'B' Troop—"

Peter grinned. "Promoted me, haven't you?"

" 'Spike'?" Peter repeated, puzzled.

"One of the troop laundresses," the girl sniffed. "My, you *are* ig—. Sorry. Ma Simmons makes grand cookies. Well, I've got to get out of here. 'Bye." She waved and ran.

Peter called his thanks after her.

Cookies! Humph! She was only a child after all.

He turned to hug the black horse at the fence—his horse now.

8: OF ARMS AND THE MAN

I

"THE trouble with this Army is—"

First Sergeant Smith muttered the first line of the soldier's traditional and eternal plaint. Innumerable soldiers have chanted it countless times since the first army was formed. Of the ancient character of the rite, the former professor bending over his table in the orderly room of "K" Troop was well aware. He also knew that those who wore the three-stripes-and-diamond chevron of his grade were supposed to be above soldier's grouches. Nor was he ignorant that one of the troubles with the Army, most frequently mentioned by the rank and file, was first sergeants. Nevertheless, as he made out his fatigue details for the day, he went on with the formula.

"The trouble with this Army," he repeated and finished, "is too much shovel and too little carbine."

He was right, and the shovel he referred to was not employed for digging trenches but ditches. All manner of non-military tasks were heaped on the garrisons of the frontier posts, so that there was never time in their waking hours for the necessary training and scouting and patrolling of Indians frequently on the warpath. The Army dug ditches and wells and built barracks because Congress allotted it no funds for civilian help. Hostile Indian tribes were not a national menace.

After the Civil War—as had happened before and would again in the history of the United States—the Army was conveniently forgotten and neglected. So, in the Southwest and West, settlers were shot and lanced and hacked to death by red raiders, women were dragged off into miserable captivity, and the brains of babies were dashed out against walls of burning cabins, since not enough troops were available to protect all. And when soldiers, veterans or recruits insufficiently trained, fell in obscure prairie skirmishes serving their country, that country seemed seldom to notice or to care.

Peter Shannon was luckier than most recruits. He was a good horseman before he enlisted. In the average cavalry regiment there was no time for instruction in equitation. Unhappy rookies, who had never ridden before, had to climb aboard a rough-gaited steed and trot off on a thirty-mile Indian chase, learning to ride en route. There was little or no opportunity for target practice because of the constant fatigue details.

But the 4th Cavalry was exceptional. Mackenzie cut fatigues to a minimum and drove officers and enlisted men hard, demanding drill and strict discipline. All of the hardships and even less of the few comforts and the little recreation in the lot of a border command—such was the rule in the 4th. Some men broke under the strain and deserted. The rest developed a stoical endurance and a fierce pride that they were tough enough to take it. Out of them Mackenzie forged the tempered steel weapon that was his regiment.

Peter's own training in the profession of arms wore him every day to the point of sheer exhaustion. Sergeant Smith first turned him and a group of other recruits over to the sabre instructor. Sergeant Pinchon, a fiery little Frenchman with mustache and goatee, closely resembled Napoleon III. He would have been called Master of the Sword in the old Dragoons, and he deserved that title. But when he appeared before his recruit detachment, his aspect as a *beau sabreur* was marred by two beautiful, black eyes.

He brought his recruits to attention and glared at them out of his empurpled orbs.

"So, *mes enfants,* I come to teach you the sabre," he

snapped. "Will you give me the attention? But no, I respond for you. Instead, you will be wondering who have presented the sergeant with the shiners. So first I tell you and be finish with it.

"There has been war in Europe. *La belle France* has by miserable chance been vanquished by Prussians. It happen there is some of that people in this regiment. In our band is a species of cow who is called Sergeant Seidlitz. As I pass his barrack he take his horn and to insult me play at me *Die Wacht Am Rhine*. Bah!

"I demand, *mes enfants,* shall I, a man of spirit, then remain tranquil. *Jamais!* I halt, I face him. I chant at him our song so splendid, *La Marseillaise*. And what does he do, that one? He only blows more. I sing louder. He then emits that music so miserable with force major.

"*Hélas!* The horn it is more powerful than the voice. I am drown out. It is time to attack. Having not my sabre at my side, I kick him where he not like it. He strike me in the eyes, where you see. I seize his horn. With it I strike him on the head. Is it the little horn like the trumpet? But no! Happily it is the big horn—the tuba. Sergeant Seidlitz he is now in hospital.

"*C'est tout*. So much for that. *Attention!* Draw sabre. *En garde*."

He drilled them to a frazzle. He made them perform the *moulinet*—swinging the sabre in a windmill-like arc to supple the wrist—until Peter was certain his arm was about to drop off. He taught them parries but insisted vehemently on offensive rather than defensive action. Each skillful attack, he told them, is at the same time a parry. And he pounded into them that they must use the point, not the edge.

"La pointe, toujours la pointe!" he cried. "For why? It arrive first—long before the blow with the edge—when you make the charge. You say it arrives not before a bullet from the revolvaire? Bah! Ten thousand times bah!"

Eyes flashing at the recruit who had mentioned a revolver, drawn sabre thrust out to the right, the little sergeant looked to Peter like a composite of all the swashbuckling swordsmen in all the romances he had ever read. Pinchon's legs were bowed as if gripping a horse he was about to ride into the fray. He fired the imaginations of his pupils, for the day of crashing cavalry charges was not yet done. The Civil War had abounded in them, and the recent Franco-Prussian War had seen such terrific cavalry combats as the Battles of Vionville and Mars le Tour. Sergeant Pinchon flung forward his weapon into the position of charge sabre.

"The sabre—*l'arme blanche!"* he exclaimed, his face alight. "Without it the cavalry is like the body without the soul. It is the sabre and the hope some day to flesh it in the foe that sustains us. Let our sabres drink deep in many a fight! Nevaire let them rust in their scabbards, or glory is lost forever. Ah, that desire so ferocious to close headlong with the enemy! It is the desire of the cavalryman of all ages. It is the desire which the sabre, and the sabre alone, can satisfy!"

Peter and the other recruits, catching some of his enthusiasm waited, breathing harder. But the sergeant fell silent—then stirred like a man awakening from a dream. He sighed and regarded the awkward squad, their sabres clutched like carving knives, with infinite disgust.

"Return—sabre," he commanded. "Into the scabbard, not the trouser leg, stupid. For today, *assez*. Dismiss."

II

Other instructors naturally favored the weapons they taught and discounted the sabre. Sergeant Hanks, a tall Tennessean, addressed Peter and the rest with gravity on the subject of his specialty.

"Sure the sabre's handy when yore out of ammunition. And y' can toast hardtack on it over a campfire, if Pinchon ain't lookin'. Revolver's good enough as a popgun. But it's the carbine you really knock 'em over with.

"This here Springfield's a good gun. Be better if 'twas a magazine rifle, but repeaters ain't issued. Y' can go buy one if y' got the money but y' likely ain't or y' wouldn't be in the Army. Anyways, thank yore stars 'tain't a muzzle-loader like we had in the War. Caused trouble, them guns did, when a soldier got a mite rattled in action. After Gettysburg they picked up thousands of muzzle-loaders with from three to ten loads—cartridge and ball—rammed home in the barr'l. One of 'em had twenty-three loads in. Know what'd happen to a feller that fired one o' them? She'd blow up kersmack in his face. He'd never have to do no more shavin'. He wouldn't have no more whiskers and, so fur as that goes, no more face.

"That's what'll happen to you re-cruits if y' stopper up the muzzle of this here car-bine with a greased rag to keep out the rain or let it git full o' sand.

"Recollect y' got only one shot at a time with this carbine. Make it good. Don't never pull yore trigger. Squeeze it. And take yore time. Don't matter if a bunch of Injuns is gallopin' down on yuh, whoopin' and yellin'. Line up yore sights on one of 'em's chist. Squeeze off yore shot, and that's taps for one Injun and likely the charge, too. They won't keep comin' agin good, steady shootin'.

"What's that y' say? Ain't a revolver better at close quarters? Why let 'em git thar? I'm going to l'arn you to shoot this here car-bine prone, sittin', kneelin', standin', and from off a hoss, so nobody gits to close quarters like y' call 'em, and t'ell with yore popguns!"

Corporal Rick instructed the recruit squad in the revolver. Though he disliked him heartily, Peter had to admit the fellow knew his subject. As Pinchon and Hanks had extolled their favorite arm, so Rick praised his. Undeniably the .44 calibre Army model Colt was an admirable weapon. Even cocked by hand (double action would not be introduced until 1877), it could put six heavy slugs of lead into a mark with incredible speed. Peter, hefting his, knew he held the power of life and death in his palm.

He felt Rick's hard gaze on him. "You, Shannon," the non-com barked. "You pointed that gun at me. Don't matter whether it's empty or not. I'm reporting you for it. That'll teach the lot of you never to point a gun at anybody you don't mean to shoot."

His small mouth curved in a malicious smile. "Well," he said, "maybe there *is* somebody you'd like to shoot. Better not try, though."

He spun his Colt by the trigger-guard like a gunman. Then he whirled and, with seeming casualness, fired six times at the mark, a small square of paper fastened to a cactus. Five bullet holes appeared, grouped close to the target's center.

"There you are," Rick boasted. "At fifty yards, too. I'll do my best with you dumb rookies but none of you'll ever be able to hit anything smaller than a horse at over twenty-five yards.

"Just the same, the Colt's your best bet. No Injun's going to wait around for you to pot him with a carbine. When a Comanche brave comes riding down on you with a long lance, what good's your sabre? Pull your six-shooter and throw some lead into his red belly."

The revolver-advocate recruit was emboldened to speak up with: "That's what I've been a-sayin' right along."

"Shut up," Rick ordered. "What do you know about it? You prob'ly haven't got the gumption to shoot a man, red or white. Neither has Shannon. But he's beginning to think he'd kind of like to, aren't you, Shannon?"

Peter returned the corporal's shrewd and insinuating wink with a narrowed look and said nothing. But that was exactly what he had been thinking. And it was an unpleasant, disturbing thought that you might come to hate a man enough to want to kill him. He would have no compunctions about killing Indians. They were the enemy, and he had already fought them for his life that day at the wagon train. But to feel murderous toward a fellow-soldier, no matter how much he taunted you—that was not right, that would not do.

Peter stopped gritting his teeth. He managed to grin at Corporal Rick. That, the other had not expected. For a moment his too-handsome face was a picture of disconcertion and disappointment. Peter grinned again, more broadly.

III

In any event, Peter was left no time for brooding and a private feud. Drillmasters put him through long, hot hours of dismounted and mounted drill, of guard and outpost duty. Peter's quick ear soon learned to recognize the many trumpet calls, but he still was not taught to play the instrument which Quartermaster Sergeant Connors called "the deadliest weepon iv thim all." Later Corporal-Trumpeter

Elliot would instruct him. First he must become the trooper, then the trumpeter.

Best of all was the instruction given by First Sergeant Smith. That born teacher took particular pains with Peter, well above the average recruit in intelligence and education. Smith tied all the other instruction together for him, showing how each weapon had its place, how a cavalryman must be able to handle all three competently. Also he coached the young trooper on the academic studies which Peter had promised his father at home to keep up.

Horses were the special love of the Top Sergeant, as they were Peter's. Already well taught by his father, Peter found he had still much to learn of horsemanship and the lore of horses from big, bearded Sam Smith.

He would never forget the day when he first rode his horse Justin. The veterinary had marked the black Morgan duty, the claw scars being healed. Very gently Peter blanketed and saddled him and stood to horse.

"Now," Sergeant Smith ordered, "tell him you're going to get up on his back. Yes, I mean it," he added, for Peter had hesitated. It hardly seemed military to talk to your horse, though he often had privately. "Horses understand," the sergeant insisted, "and this fellow needs to know what you're going to do. I've seen horses that had been jumped by a mountain lion that never could be ridden. Bucked off the best riders, and you can't blame 'em after what they'd been through."

Peter spoke in Justin's ear. Then he quietly gathered the reins and set foot in stirrup.

Smith said: "Sit down in the saddle lightly but grip tight with your knees. There may be fireworks and a balloon ascension. All right. Mount."

Peter obeyed. As the horse felt his weight, he trembled

violently and his eyes rolled as a dreadful memory flooded back into his brain. He began to gather himself and arch his back for running buck-jumps. It was touch and go.

Peter sat still and easily in the saddle. He spoke: "It's me. It's all right, old fellow." He rubbed Justin's neck. Gradually the trembling ceased. The rider moved his mount off at a slow walk.

Sergeant Smith sighed with relief. "That decides it," he said. "I was afraid we had an outlaw. Instead we've got a cavalry mount and a fine one."

The sergeant saw to it that Peter taught Justin to respond both to the reins laid against his neck and to the pressure of his rider's legs. The time would come when Peter would want to be able simply to loop the reins over an arm and have his hands free for arms or trumpet.

"You probably never knew when you struggled with your Latin—with Caesar's *Commentaries,*" the ex-professor observed—"that old Julius C. was a fine horseman and was especially renowned for the feats he performed on a bridle-wise horse.

"Always remember this. In training a horse, don't use only the fear of punishment, but reward him whenever he does well. Even the dry, precise drill manual waxes human when it speaks of the cavalryman's horse. It tells the trooper to 'make much of him.' But that's a passage I don't think I need to recommend to you with this Morgan of yours."

The older man had not failed to sense the current of affection running between the boy and the black horse. The average trooper was fond of his mount, but this seemed an even stronger tie than usual. For an instant, the sergeant's eyes took on a sad expression. Too often had he seen such close companionships of frontier service broken by an Indian bullet that dropped a troop horse or emptied his saddle.

"One thing more, young Shannon," his preceptor went on. "You must master yourself before you can master a horse. Another of the ancients you may have toiled over in school, old Xenophon—"

Peter interposed. "I know. The general who led his army of 10,000 Greeks through the enemy and down to the sea."

"The same. And he did not write only the *Anabasis* but excellent works on horses and cavalry. Listen to this." The Sergeant drew out his notebook and flipped its pages. "Xenophon wrote this about 400 B.C., but horses and men who understand them have not changed.

" 'Never to lose one's temper with the horse is a good precept and an excellent habit,' " he read. " 'To lose one's temper is unreasonable and makes one do things one can but afterwards regret. When a horse shows fright of some object and refuses to go near it, one must make him feel that he has nothing to fear, and the more especially so if the horse be a high-couraged one. The rider will do well himself to walk up to such object and touch it, subsequently to lead the horse up to it. Those riders who force the horse by the use of the whip will only increase his terror, for he will imagine that the pain he feels is inflicted upon him by the object that frightens him.' "

As the First Sergeant finished speaking, a trumpet call, sharp and insistent, sounded.

"Boots and Saddles," Peter identified it.

Ordinarily, the call was a summons to mounted drill or some other mounted formation. But none was scheduled at this hour. This time it meant action.

9: MIDNIGHT, CANYON BLANCO

I

YOU acted more or less automatically, doing all the things you had to do, almost without thinking, but doing them well and forgetting no details. Peter began to realize it as he obeyed the trumpeted summons of *Boots and Saddles*. That was the reason for the hot hours of drill, all the monotonous repetition, the fussy insistence of drillmasters on everything being done just so. In time it made a soldier of you.

That was training, and the end of training was battle, and now battle lay ahead. Peter, saddling up Justin, could not doubt it from the snatches of talk he heard along the picket line.

"Comanches are out again. . . . Raided a ranch and ran off a lot of stock. . . . Chief Quanah? Sounds like him. . . . Hear General Mac says he's goin' to run 'em down this time, if the regiment has to ride over the en-tire State o' Texas. . . . Get that, you rookies? Better bring along some pillows to put in your pants."

Peter grinned and made fast his cinch strap. The black Morgan turned his head and looked at him questioningly out of his large, lustrous eyes.

"Yes," his rider softly answered the look, "we're off, and it's the real thing, I think. We're going into action."

He led out, took his place in the line of file closers of his troop and stood to horse. Captain Bone, a newly-attached lieutenant named Carter, and the First Sergeant made a rapid but thorough inspection. "Prepare to mount," came the troop commander's voice. "Mount." As one man, the troopers thrust upward in stirrups, swung right legs over cantles and settled in their saddles.

Eight troops of the 4th Cavalry formed to march: A, B, D, F, G, H, K, and L. Yonder two companies of the 11th Infantry dressed ranks. Peter gazed over at them with none of the traditional contempt of mounted for foot troops. His father's stories had taught him to respect infantry, and Sergeant Smith had declared that Indians would rather tackle cavalry, horse against horse, than charge a rock-firm company of doughboys.

There milled a score of Tonkawa scouts, good trailers, mortal foes of the Comanches. Packed and ready, the wagon train waited, with it a herd of pack-mules to be used when the going became too rough for wheels.

A trumpet sounded. "Fours right," and "K" Troop moved into column and across the parade ground to its place in the blue array. Over toward Officers' Row, a small figure in a gingham dress was waving good-by so vigorously that her pigtails bobbed up and down. Peter, being in ranks, naturally ignored her; besides, she undoubtedly was waving to the regiment, not to him.

Sally Ann looked excited, didn't she? Well, you couldn't blame the sprig. It must be thrilling for a girl to watch troops march off on a campaign. Peter had to acknowledge to himself that his own blood was tingling.

Beat of hundreds of hooves and the creak of saddle leather. The vital warmth of a trusted mount gripped by his knees. Pressure of the strap of his carbine sling over his shoulder, and the reassuring tug of sabre and revolver on his belt. Guidons, half red, half white, flaunting their forked tails in the breeze. A long column of cavalry flowing on steadily and he, Peter Shannon, a part of it, his dream, long-dreamt, come true.

II

They marched on steadily. Twice, quicksand streams, with deep banks and no regular fords, delayed the column but not for long. Spirits were high. Now and again a troop raised a song that was a favorite of the regiment.

"Come home, John.
Don't stay long.
Come home soon
To your own Chick-a-biddy."

Halt, bivouac, sleep, break camp, march on. So it went. Still the "Tonk" scouts up ahead struck no Comanche trail. The column marched past huge herds of buffalo and risked the sound of shots to kill a few for fresh meat. At length Mackenzie, in order to speed the pursuit, established a supply camp, corralled the wagons and left the two infantry companies as a guard. The cavalry pushed on with pack-mules loaded with rations and ammunition.

Lance Elliot dropped by Peter's side. "Aren't we ever going to strike their trail?" the latter asked him.

"We'll find them—or they'll find us," answered the former Confederate. "I hear this is a band of Quohada Comanches under Quanah, and Quanah Parker is always ready for a fight."

"Quanah *Parker?* Why, that name's half white."

"So's its owner," Elliot declared. As they rode on together, the trumpeter told the dramatic story of Cynthia Ann Parker.

"She was a pretty little thing, they say," he related in his soft, Southern voice. "Blue eyes and cornsilk-yellow hair. She was only a young girl when it happened—back in the '30's it was, I reckon. Her father, a Texas settler, with a few other men and their women and children, held a strong stockade, called Parker's Fort, on one of the forks of the Brazos. Along came a party of Comanches and Kiowas one day with a flag of truce, saying they were friendly and wanted to make a treaty. Parker was rash enough to believe 'em and let 'em in.

"You can guess what happened. The Indians massacred all the men and some of the women and children. They tied up Cynthia Ann and other survivors, beat them, and stamped on them in a scalp dance, waving the bloody trophies they had just taken. A chief named Nacoma claimed Cynthia Ann as his captive. The Texas authorities did their best to find and ransom her, but she'd vanished without a trace.

"A good twenty years later, a captain of Texas Rangers met a Comanche chieftain on the plains hereabouts. They fought—single combat—a fight to the finish." Elliot's eyes glowed as he spoke. "The chief drove an arrow into the Ranger's horse. His next arrows very nearly got the rider. The Ranger couldn't fire. It was all he could do to sit his horse, rearing and plunging, wild with pain. At last the captain got his revolver into action. He hit the Comanche three times, once in the right arm and twice through the body. But that Indian wasn't doing any surrendering. His last act before a final bullet finished him off was a vicious thrust at his enemy with a lance, gripped in his unwounded left hand.

"More Rangers came up. They galloped after and caught the chief's squaw, who had been close to escaping. Yes, it was Cynthia Ann Parker."

Peter said: "She sure must have been glad to get back to her own people again."

"No, it was too late. It had been too long. She had borne the chief three children. She'd gone the whole way and turned Indian. All the rest of her life she had to be watched carefully to prevent her going back to her tribe. One of her sons was Quanah. He became chief in his father's place. As crafty and daring as old Nacoma and as valiant. That's Quanah Parker."

"The fellow we're scouting for now," Peter added.

"Or who's scouting for us," Elliot amended. He straightened in his saddle, and there was a gleam in his eyes again. "Some day I hope to meet him personally."

Peter thought: Knights must have looked like that when they threw down the gauntlet and challenged somebody to mortal combat.

Upraised hands forward in the column signaled a halt. Orders came to go into bivouac.

A stream flowed along one side of the camp site chosen. Bluffs rose abruptly on the other. They would furnish protection in case a norther blew up. But this was a pocket valley—Canyon Blanco it was called. As one squadron followed another in there to encamp, it was crowded with men and horses. First Sergeant Sam Smith kept gazing about him. Peter saw the veteran frown and slightly shake his head.

Word was passed that fires could be lit. It meant hot food for the tired troopers and warmth against the chill of the night. But again Sergeant Smith shook his head in foreboding.

"See to your lariats when you stake out your horse," he ordered the troop. "If I find a man whose picket pin isn't driven in deep, he's going to regret it."

Peter pounded the iron pin down into the ground and tethered his mount to it securely. Not that Justin was likely to stray. If he did, he would return at his master's whistle. But orders were orders.

III

Midnight and black as ink. Here and there, the embers of a campfire glowed faintly. The camp was quiet except for men snoring in their blankets and the *champ-click* of horses grazing at the end of their lariats.

Then the Comanches struck, riding in through the masking foothills. Whooping, yelling, clanging bells and dragging dried buffalo robes, they came—making a terrifying, unearthly din. Dazed troopers wrenched themselves out of their heavy sleep, groped for their weapons. Carbines spurted red and banged, as the rear squadron went into action.

"Get to your horses!" The voices of the officers and noncoms were hoarse and urgent. They knew the purpose of

Then the Comanches struck . . . whooping, clanging

the racket the attacking Indians were making. —a stampede. Running off all the horses of the 4th would leave it in a desperate situation—might even mean disaster.

The disciplined regiment steadied. Troopers ran to obey the shouted commands. But the horses and mules—600 of them—were snorting and plunging about in terror, straining with all their strength at the lariats that held them. They groaned and trembled pitifully in a frenzy of fright. Now lariats binding them began to snap like pistol shots. Iron picket pins, wrenched loose, hurtled through the air, more deadly missiles than any of the Indian bullets whistling by. Men grabbed for the dragging lines. Some were forced to loose them, as tugging animals dashed away, and skin was rope-burned from the palms of hands. Others held on and were hauled under the lashing heels of panic-stricken brutes.

Commands still carried over the tumult. "Every man to his lariat! Stand by your horses!"

It was Justin's four white stockings that guided Peter to him. As terrorized as the rest, the Morgan was making frantic efforts to break away. Peter, risking the hooves of the rearing horse, hauled on the line, hand over hand. Justin jerked back with all his might. His master clung on, talking soothingly. Gradually, the familiar, well-loved voice exerted its spell. At length Justin, sweating and shaking, stood still and let himself be saddled.

Peter, climbing up on his horse's back, knew the blessed relief the cavalryman feels at being once more mounted. Other troopers also had succeeded in recovering animals. Squads of horsemen were being organized for pursuit down the canyon, while dismounted men were pushing up the ridge as skirmishers. Peter, unable to find anyone to ask for orders, helped other men catch and saddle their mounts.

He was thus engaged when he heard his name called.

"You, Shannon."

Peter recognized Corporal Rick's harsh tones. From the Morgan's back he looked down at the shadowy figure approaching. Rick was limping, apparently had lost his mount.

"Report to Sergeant Smith up on the ridge, Shannon," he ordered.

"Right, Corporal." Peter gathered his reins.

"No you don't, Rookie. Not mounted. Dismounted. Give me that plug of yours. Lost mine. My squad's detailed for the chase."

Peter stared down at the other's insolent face, clearer under the graying light.

Rick snapped: "Get down off that horse and be quick about it."

It was, Peter realized, "the lawful order of a non-commissioned officer, given in performance of his duties." Without a word he dismounted and handed over Justin's reins. Unslinging his carbine, he hurried on up the ridge.

IV

Apparently, the Comanches did not care to tackle the parties deployed along the ridge but had faded away with the approach of dawn. However, the position was held a little longer to play safe.

A German-American corporal, who had been in charge of one of the outposts overrun in the savages' first onslaught, began telling his story in broken English.

"I vas lying down ven a shot I hear. I shoomp up. I dry grab mein bicket pin but dee horses roosh py. Next ding I know dee Injuns dey ride all ofer me. I raise mein carbine to mein preast. Der piggest Injun I shoot. He stagger, he fall almost and he deesappear in dee dark."

Peter laughed with the rest but his heart was not in it. He was worried. Finally, to his relief, his detachment was marched back to camp. It still was a scene of havoc—horses and lines in a frightful tangle—equipment strewn about everywhere.

Score a surprise and partial triumph for the Comanches. Seventy of the regiment's best horses and mules were gone. Mackenzie had lost a fine, gray pacer; other officers lamented valuable chargers. Peter, reflecting how lucky he had been to hold on to Justin, hurried in search of Rick and the horse. He found only the former, talking to a trooper named Gregg. Rick looked dusty and disgruntled.

"I'll take my horse now, Corporal," Peter said curtly.

"Take him and be hanged," Rick growled. "How you ever rode him I don't know. That black devil bucked me off—me that was riding when you was still on a hobbyhorse in the nursery! He tossed *me!*"

Peter tried to smother a grin. Rick saw it and flushed with anger.

"Funny, ain't it? Well, go laugh with your bucking broncho—if you can find him."

Peter's face went white. "What do you mean? Where is he?" he demanded.

"How do I know? After he piled me, he lit out. Probably joined all the rest of our missing nags. 'Smatter? Think I ought of run after him?"

Trooper Gregg interposed. "Look here, Corp. Kind of hard on the lad, ain't you?"

The look in Peter's eyes had sent Rick's hand to his revolver butt. But Peter only turned and walked away.

"Tough to lose a hoss you're fond of," Gregg said. "Guess you just don't feel it, Rick. Now if it was a gal of yours was swiped, you sure would be riled. Wonder where the lad's gone to? Wouldn't be fool enough to go wandering off in Comanche country lookin' for that hoss, would he?"

"Might," Rick answered indifferently.

10: DEVIL TAKES HINDMOST

I

Two powerful emotions had gripped Peter. A deep affection for the lost Morgan, above and beyond the duty of a cavalryman toward his horse, and a burning hate for Rick. The first had proved stronger. Find Justin he must. Rick could be dealt with later.

He strode blindly through the camp. The few who noted

his haste assumed he was an orderly carrying a field message. Still unnoticed—outposts were being called in preparatory to a march—he hurried out of the canyon and was soon hidden in the draws and arroyos cutting the plain.

Gradually, he began to think more rationally. In what direction had Justin run after he bucked Rick off? Peter had no idea. He halted and made himself consider how futile it was to scour the country on foot in search of a runaway horse. Almost had he decided to return when he caught sight of a trail of hoof marks—shod hooves.

He took it up eagerly. It might be any cavalry horse or even a Comanche pony, some of which were shod. But it could be his horse. That was enough. Peter took up the trail.

Four, five miles, and more he put behind him. He grew hot and tired. It began to dawn on him that he would be turned in as a deserter. He was "absent from his post of duty in the face of the enemy." Under the Articles of War, the penalty for that was death. But he had an explanation for his absence, hadn't he? . . . Yes, and there seldom, if ever, was a deserter who hadn't. Courts-martial were inclined to be highly sceptical of deserters' stories.

Nevertheless, dogged and unwavering, Peter followed the horse's trail.

How foolhardy he was to wander alone through Comanche country, still had not occurred to him. Nor did it until, as he was about to enter a draw, he suddenly perceived a feathered head and a copper-colored body streaked with war paint.

Peter drew back hastily and took cover. Fortunately, the Indian, being fully occupied, had not observed him. Peter, scouting up to the rim, discovered that the draw was blind as he gazed downward through a cleft between rocks. Then he saw what was engaging the warrior's attention. In the closed end of the draw a black horse with four white feet was cornered—Justin!

Peter pulled his carbine from its sling socket, poked it slowly through the cleft, then reluctantly withdrew it. He could not risk a shot at the Indian with the horse in the line of fire as he now was. He could only watch and wait.

The black Morgan was lathered and dust-covered but still saddled and bridled. Clearly, he did not like this red man's closing in on him. Yet he was cornered and he knew it. Naturally docile, he let his bridle be grasped.

But the next action he would not brook. With astonishing speed and agility the Indian had vaulted on to his back. Like a cat, Peter thought as he peered down.

"Like a cat." The similarity must have struck the horse no less forcibly. Again an onrush of fearful memories of that ride by the spitting, clawing mountain lion came sweeping back. No beloved voice soothed him as when his master had first mounted him. He heard only hoarse, guttural cries and felt a quirt cut viciously into his belly.

Justin jumped, whirled and began to buck madly. He bunched those white feet and dashed across the draw in great, soaring leaps. He came down stiff-legged in bone-jarring landings. He twisted and "sunfished."

Peter barely kept himself from cheering. This, he chuckled to himself, was what must have happened to Rick. But this time Justin had a different rider—a Comanche, a born horseman. The Morgan redoubled his efforts. Still the brave stuck on. He had broken many a wild mustang, riding bareback with only a rope surcingle.

Yet, this was a lion-scarred horse. Justin became a blazing, black streak of furious action. It was too much for the

Comanche. He was catapulted off and hit the prairie with a thud.

In an instant, he had bounded to his feet. A good horse was a coveted possession of a warrior, but an outlaw like this was good only as horsemeat. The Comanche unslung his bow, whipped an arrow from his quiver and notched it. Circling around Justin to reach a vantage point for his shot, he drew his bowstring taut.

There was very little time. Peter, carbine shoved through the cleft again, realized that. Even so, Sergeant Hanks' drawled instructions kept beating into his consciousness, controlling his actions.

"Take yore time, son. Hurry an' y' shore will miss. Line up yore targit in yore sights. Git yore front sight squar' in that thar v-notch of the rear sight and balance yore bullseye on top the front 'un. Suck in yore breath some—not too much, though—an' hold it. Take up the play in yore trigger an' squeeze, never pull it, and afore y' know it—"

Bang! The carbine crashed before Peter knew it was going off. That was how Sergeant Hanks said it ought to be. And what he said would happen to a live target, if you had held on steady, was happening down there in the draw.

The Comanche had dropped his bow. On his broad, coppery back appeared a red splotch, just below the left shoulder blade. His knees folded and he fell forward on his face and lay still.

Quickly, Peter reloaded, as the sergeant had taught him. That shot would bring any Indians in the vicinity, and there were likely to be plenty. Knowing he must corral Justin and get out of there, he ran down to the mouth of the draw.

Just as he reached it, the Morgan horse tore past him with a thunder of hooves.

The Comanche whipped an arrow from his quiver

"Justin!" his master shouted despairingly after him. He gave the shrill whistle the horse knew so well. But the galloping black never hesitated in his headlong flight.

Private Shannon, Troop "K," 4th U.S. Cavalry, stood still, carbine in the crook of his arm. He was only a recruit but he was well aware of the grim outlook for a dismounted trooper far from his outfit in strange and hostile territory. If thirst didn't get you, the Comanches or the Kiowas would.

His eyes scanned the prairie. Oddly, the dust cloud marking the Morgan's flight had not decreased with distance. On the contrary, it was growing. And silhouetted against it was a black shape, trotting back toward him.

A glimpse of the master he loved as he raced by. The sound of the whistle he was trained to answer. These had been enough for the faithful and intelligent animal, once their import, delayed by his panicky impulse to escape, had reached his brain. These and all they meant to him had drawn him back.

II

A detachment from "G" and "K" Troops, ordered out on a scout that morning, had ridden only a few miles when they sighted a dozen Comanches running off some of the 4th's stampeded mounts. Their luck was good—suspiciously so, they realized shortly. Riding hard, they pursued until they were halted by a long, narrow arroyo barring their advance. Only a few of the horses could be made to leap the gap. The bulk of the detachment swung to the right to ride around.

Lieutenant Carter, a sergeant, and four men galloped on after the Indians, who vanished into a second ravine two miles further along. No sooner had the pursuing cavalrymen entered than they reined in to a sudden halt. They had been led into an ambuscade. The ridge beyond was swarming with Comanche horsemen. Whooping, they fanned out and rode down on the trapped soldiers.

"Dismount," came Carter's command. Their horses were tired. It seemed best to try to hold off the Indians until the rest of the detachment came up. His men were all veterans and armed with Spencer repeating carbines. Yet, as the lieutenant saw more and more warriors gathering on the ridge, the desperate realization came to him that the detachment was not strong enough to fight its way through to him. His only hope was that Mackenzie would hear the firing and ride with the regiment to the rescue.

Sergeant Jenkins called to him. Dust to the rear. The detachment was coming up, after all. No . . . it was only one trooper. He came, riding fast to escape the Comanches closing in on his flank. As the single horseman galloped up, Trooper Gregg identified him.

"Young Shannon out of 'K.' Went looking for a stray horse this morning an'—"

Carter called out before Peter could speak: "Take the horses and fall back toward the ravine. Now, men, deploy and open fire."

Peter rode Justin slowly to the rear, reins of the led horses, linked three and three, over his arms. Over his shoulder he stared back at the Indians, mustering for the attack as they had that bloody day at the wagon train. But here was savage might and barbaric splendor far surpassing that other occasion. Even the ponies, especially the whites, duns, and claybanks, gleamed with war paint. Along the red ranks, signal mirrors flashed in the sun. Chiefs acting as standard-bearers held aloft scalp-poles from which swung trophies of long, flowing hair. Squaws, watching from a butte, shrieked in shrill encouragement of the warriors' charge.

Peter, getting the horses under cover in the arroyo, heard the steady firing of Carter's men which checked that charge. Now the troopers came back on the run. Almost at the mouth of the arroyo, they turned and dropped prone.

"Now, men," Lieutenant Carter shouted. "Unlock your magazines, bunch your shots, pump it into 'em and make a dash for your lives! It's all we can do!"

A ringing fusillade. Into the ravine the troopers came tumbling, the right hand of one of them dripping blood. They flung themselves into their saddles, and Carter waved them forward. From their last fierce volley the Comanches had recoiled but they would soon be in hot pursuit.

Peter heard the officer calling to him as they galloped: "Aren't you a trumpeter? Where's your trumpet?" Peter called back that he was not yet trained. Carter groaned: "If you could only sound *Rally* now!"

On came the Comanches in full cry. How weary the troop horses were! They could not last much longer. However, many of the Indians' ponies were tired, too, and the pursuit strung out. But steadily and inexorably it gained and in its van, closing in at a thundering pace, rode a tall, powerful chief on a racing pony as coal-black as the Morgan.

Lieutenant Carter and Peter would never be able to forget the spectacle he presented. His magnificent war bonnet of eagle feathers streamed out behind him. Black war paint smeared the broad, fierce face beneath it, combining with a look of bloodthirsty joy to give it an utterly diabolical aspect. Sun glinted on the chief's brass earrings, on his necklace of bear's claws and on the silver ornaments of his black's bridle. Over his head he brandished a six-shooter.

"Quanah! Quanah Parker!" Carter cried.

The great war chief of the Quohada Comanches swung his pony toward the left. Over there a trooper, his mount faltering badly in its stride, was dropping back. It was Gregg.

"Lieutenant, my horse is giving out!" he yelled.

Carter swung his charger over to attempt to cover him. Both he and Peter fired their revolvers at Quanah and missed when the wily Indian zigzagged. He rode up on the doomed trooper's other side, masking their fire. Gregg was vainly tugging at his own holstered Colt when Quanah's weapon flamed at the back of his head and he toppled from his saddle, dead before he hit the ground.

Who would be the next victim? It seemed certain that the fleeing cavalrymen would be picked off one by one.

But Quanah and his band had turned and were riding off. Over a rise, Lieutenant Boehm and a detachment of scouts came galloping.

"All right, Carter, let's push 'em now," he shouted. "Mackenzie and the whole regiment are right behind us."

III

Push them they did, but Quanah and his tribesmen melted away. After them marched the 4th and caught never a glimpse of its elusive quarry. The Comanches, doubling back on their own trail, fooled even the Tonk scouts. Persistently Mackenzie drove on. Toward a plateau the long column of horses and mules climbed steadily, the ascent growing ever steeper until, at length, it was topped.

Peter stiffened in his saddle. The Morgan horse's well-shaped ears pricked forward in simultaneous recognition. They had emerged on to the *Llano Estacado*—the Staked Plain—where first they had met. Treeless, lifeless, it stretched away before them, seemingly as limitless as the ocean.

Reaching that high tableland, the 4th appeared to have ridden out of summer into winter. A bitter wind blew, prelude to a Texas norther. Without gloves or overcoats, the cavalrymen, from Mackenzie to the newest recruit, shivered as the gusts penetrated thin uniforms. Yet, on they marched, and now the glow of excitement warmed them. They had struck the trail, a broad trail, the trail of the whole Comanche village.

The 4th took up a trot, then a gallop. Now moving figures showed against the skyline—warriors, hundreds of them, massing to defend their women and children and give them time to escape with the pony herd. Here was the crisis of the campaign.

Commands came fast. Close up . . . Column of fours . . . Count off . . . Serve out extra ammunition and fill blouse pockets . . . Pack-mules into herd formation under guard of a squadron . . . Mounted skirmishers to the front and flanks. All these the regiment executed while still moving forward. Peter gathered Justin under him, felt for his sabre hilt, listened for trumpets sounding the charge.

And then the norther struck—darkness and biting wind, rain and snow, and whipping sleet, all rising to the fury of a gale. It was now or never, all or nothing.

The order that would have sent the 4th charging down on the Comanche through the storm never was given. Men and horses were worn and weary. The supply base was a hundred miles away. Once troops were committed to a mêlée in that blackness, organization and control would vanish. Yet, at stake was a brilliant, crushing victory, and there was not an officer or trooper in the regiment who did not expect the hard-driving Mackenzie to take the gamble.

Mackenzie, dismounting and assembling his regiment in the blackness to weather the norther, let the Comanches go. His was the dreadful responsibility of command. No officer worthy of his commission lightly commits men to battle and death. Mackenzie had wcighed the risk and counted the cost. There would be another time.

11: A TOKEN FOR THE TRUMPETER

I

THERE were gaps in the ranks, wounded in the wagons, and troopers on foot, when the 4th marched back to its station. It was no consolation that there would be mourning in the lodges of the Comanches. Quanah and his red warriors had struck and escaped. That amounted to defeat for the blue column, and it had been close to disaster that night in the canyon. Fortunes of war, said the 4th, and charged the fruitless campaign against experience. Tired men and horses, worn and thin, set about recuperating—"in addition to their other duties," as the Army phrase puts it.

The old routine of drill and fatigue recommenced its relentless rotation. To Peter it was welcome relief when his friend, Lance Elliot, told him after dismissal from a *Retreat* formation:

"Top Sergeant says start you tooting tomorrow, Pete. Drawn your trumpet? All right. Got plenty of wind? That's all you'll need then, but . . . oh, yes, your trumpet cord. I'll be teaching you 'sling trumpet,' 'secure trumpet,' and the rest of the manual."

"Will I really need a sling right away?" Peter asked. "Yellow worsted for it was issued me but—"

"It's not yet braided and you don't know how? Neither do I. Get the saddler to do it or one of the laundresses on Soapsuds Row."

"Well, it's already—"

"I see." Elliot smiled his slow smile. "Then march yourself right up to see the young lady, make your manners and get that cord. That's an order."

Reluctantly and slowly, Peter fetched his trumpet and walked toward the Lindsay quarters. It was just as well to see only so much of little girls. Give them any encouragement and they would be under foot all the time. And even though they were little more than babies, people started teasing you about them, ridiculous as that was. In exasperation Peter asked himself: Why did I ever let the brat get hold of that cord?

Knocking at the Lindsay's kitchen door, Peter sniffed one of the most delectable odors that had ever entered his nostrils. Ma Simmons, the stout, genial troop laundress, who also cooked for the Lindsay family, told him to come in and shoved a second pan of cookies into the oven. She had a caller, a grizzled old soldier whose eyes were watery but twinkling and whose nose bloomed red as the rose. Peter recognized him as Private "Peruna" Simmons, the perennial prisoner, known as "Persimmons" for short.

"You know Simmons here," Ma said to Peter, waving toward her visitor. "No relation to me nor ever like to be. 'Tis out of the guardhouse he is for a wonder but not for long. Soon as he steps up to the pay table and gets what money is left after fines, he'll be down at the post trader's, spending it for whiskey. And 'tis back in the clink he'll be next morning. And him an iducated man, more's the pity."

"Down with drink. Never again, say I," Persimmons vowed jovially. "Anyway, pay day is long overdue.

" 'They say some disaster
Befell the paymaster.' "

he quoted and winked at Peter.

"And what will you be after doing in the meantime?" Ma scolded. "You'll be buying that tonic on tick—that Pe-runa. The only difference between Pe-runa and likker is the label. 'Tis the Demon in disguise."

"Ah, Peruna! Good for man or beast." The old soldier sighed. "It cures every ill, from colic to corns. But I suspect it was an overdose of it put me in the guardhouse. I'm foreswearing it. Made me miss that Comanche chase."

Except that it prevented him from riding off on a campaign with his troop, the guardhouse wasn't a bad place, the veteran informed Peter. A man could shed responsibilities there. And there he had the sympathetic companionship of Old Taylor, the guardhouse dog. Once a prisoner was released and returned to duty, Old Taylor would have nothing to do with him.

"That neglect of his used to hurt my feelings," Persimmons confessed. "Then I realized that he, a dumb animal, was faithfully and wholeheartedly following the Scriptural injunction to visit the sick and those in affliction and them that have been cast into prison. The dog, young Shannon, is indeed man's best friend. Where else can man find such loyalty, such understanding? Not, I warrant you, in women."

Ma Simmons was rising in wrath when Sally Ann burst into the kitchen. She stopped short at the sight of Peter.

"Oh, it's you," she said curtly. "Never took the trouble to let me know how Justin was, did you? I should think you might have known I'd be worried about him. I finally had to go down and see for myself. That was a hard campaign, and the poor dear looks simply awful. You take good care of him or—"

"Say! You don't have to tell me to take care of my own horse. That's my business," Peter flashed.

"You bet it's your business. And if you don't do it, the Colonel will know it. Oh. I s'pose you came around for some cookies. Mrs. Simmons, please give this soldier some cookies. I promised him some once."

Peter glared at the girl. "I wouldn't eat any of your old cookies if I was starving!" he declared. He was lying like a trooper and he knew it. The difficulty was that he felt as if he *were* starving. After a long diet of bacon, beans, and hardtack, the appetizing aroma of the cookies was almost more than he could endure. He kept swallowing, for his mouth was watering frightfully.

"Don't eat any then!" Sally Ann snapped.

"Now, boys and girls—" Ma Simmons began to plead, but the girl broke in furiously:

"Well, if you didn't come for cookies, what *are* you here for then? I know very well it isn't to see me."

" 'Hell,' " murmured Persimmons softly, " 'hath no fury like a woman scorned.' "

"I came after my trumpet cord," Peter answered coldly. "Sorry I ever bothered you with it."

"Oh." Sally Ann whisked out of the kitchen and was back with the cord in two seconds. She looked for all the world as if she were about to throw it at its owner.

Private Simmons rose to his feet. The sodden old soldier had vanished and the gentleman of the old school he once had been stood in his place.

"Sally Ann Lindsay," he ordered with quiet authority, "finish the task you accepted. Attach the cord to the trumpet." He took the instrument from Peter and handed it to her. Fuming, the major's daughter obeyed. She fastened the triple-braided cord neatly to the rings and extended the trumpet toward Peter. Sullenly, he accepted it.

"Your manners, sir," Persimmons reminded.

"Sorry." Peter reddened. "Thank you very much," he told the braider frostily and formally. Hastily, he slung the trumpet so that it hung at his left side.

Sally Ann stamped a small foot. She walked straight up to the boy, put her arms around him to sweep the cord over his head and reslung the trumpet correctly. In the moment she stood there close to him, Peter stared fascinated into brown eyes smouldering with resentment toward him. Her red lips were parted—she was still breathing fast. A tendril of soft hair lightly brushed his cheek.

So confused he scarcely knew what he was doing, Peter mumbled his thanks again and stumbled out the door. Why, when that girl got angry, she was actually pretty. And when she stood so close, thought Peter, a strange turmoil rioting within him, she didn't seem like such a little girl after all.

II

It wasn't easy, the trumpet. You couldn't simply blow into it because all that then emerged was a futile *whoosh.* You pressed your tongue against the back of your upper teeth and pronounced the syllable *tu,* as you blew. The air thus released made your lips vibrate and the trumpet sound. Corporal-Trumpeter Elliot instructed:

"What you do, Pete, is press the mouthpiece against your lips and go through the motions of spitting into it, inelegant as that may seem. Only you blow instead. Until you toughen up your lip muscles, you'll not accomplish much. To sound higher notes, press the mouthpiece tighter against your lips. Now try it."

Peter managed a few discordant squawks. "Gosh!" he sighed. "Where did you ever learn, Lance?"

"When I rode with Jeb Stuart," declared his friend, eyes lighting with the memory, "officers in the Confederate cavalry sometimes carried trumpets. Came in handy if your trumpeter was lost or killed. There was music wherever the General went. He had a grand banjo player named Joe Sweeny. The General's personal minstrel, you might call him. Played for dances Saturday nights and hymns on Sunday. When we went raiding, Jeb and his staff would ride singing at the head of the column, Joe twanging away on his banjo, trumpets chiming in. We made the echoes ring, I tell you, with *Old Joe Hooker, Won't You Come Out of the Wilderness* and *Alabama Gals* and *Sweet Evelina.*

" '*Haec olim meminisse juvabit,*' as they taught me at Princeton. 'These things hereafter will be a joy to remember,' " Elliot said. But his eyes had saddened with remembrances of a gallant leader killed in action.

Practice, practice, practice on the trumpet, day after day. So it went, and Peter could not see that he was making any progress. Only occasionally could he produce a sound recognizable as a musical note, mostly he emitted squeals, squeaks, grunts, and dismal groans. Elliot was a patient, an excellent teacher. He alternated technique with the manual of the trumpet and instruction on a trumpeter's posts and duties.

" 'As the duties of a trumpeter quite often cause him to become more conspicuous than other members of his company or regiment,' " Elliot quoted, " 'he should for this reason always endeavor to maintain a neat and soldierly appearance.' "

He made Peter learn to sing all the calls before attempting to play them—taught him to remember that drill signals for movements to the right always ran up the scale, if to the left, down. Notes ascended for *Mount,* descended for *Dismount.* Signals for changes of gait were all on the same sound and each imitated the tempo of the gait it ordered.

Words set to the notes of calls helped your memory a lot. There was First Call and its ironic promise:

Fall in, ye poor devils, as fast as ye can.
And when ye get tired, I'll rest ye again.

And *Sick Call,* whose summons was especially well answered at posts where malaria was rife.

Doctor Jones says, Doctor Jones says,
Come get your quinine, quinine, quinine.
Come get your genuine qui-i-nine.

That call was even more fully attended when the word got around that the quinine had run out and doses of whiskey were being given instead.

There was Mess Call, always popular but far too often disillusioning, Army cooks and rations being what they were.

Soupy, soupy, soup, without a single bean.
Coffee, coffee, coff, without a bit of cream.
Porky, porky, pork, without a streak of lean.

Lively, lilting *Reveille,* borrowed from the French Army, like so many others of our trumpet calls, was as difficult to blow as it was to obey on dark, cold mornings.

I can't get 'em up, I can't get 'em up,
I can't get 'em up in the morning.
I can't get 'em up, I can't get 'em up,
I can't get 'em up at all.
The corporal's worse then the private.
The sergeant's worse than the corporal.
The lieutenant's worse than the sergeant,
And the captain's the worst of all.

Because of the fearful sounds he was making and because, as a result, he had been ordered to practice some distance away from the post, Peter never had any company but his instructor. But one day a visitor arrived. Old Taylor, the guardhouse dog, trotted up and sat down at the feet of the novice with an air of solicitude and resignation. Plainly he had come to stay for the duration of the practice.

Peter demanded: "Say, what does this visitation mean? That I'm such a terrible trumpeter that Old Taylor knows they're going to throw me in the guardhouse?"

Elliot laughed. "Not quite that bad. Old Taylor always rallies 'round when he hears a new trumpeter learning. That dog is the soul of sympathy. He hangs around the guardhouse to be solace to prisoners, most of 'em not deserving any. He's here for the same reason. From the sounds he hears, he thinks you're suffering. He'll be doggoned if he isn't going to suffer with you, no matter how much your horn-tooting hurts his ears."

"Aw, come on, Lance."

"You'll see. To him it's just like sitting up with a sick friend. He'll be here every day now till your trumpeting begins to sound human."

And Old Taylor, long bloodhound ears and jowls drooping, a world of pity in his large, mournful eyes, never failed to be present for practice.

Surprisingly there came still another visitor. First Sergeant Sam Smith rode out one day when Peter was tooting away alone. He was riding his horse, Big Bill, and leading Justin.

"I want you to begin to practice mounted now," he told Peter. "You must be able to sound calls at a trot or gallop. And your horse must learn to recognize and obey calls. Most of the troop horses can." He swung out of the saddle. "Now let me hear what you can do, young Shannon. Try *Mess Call.* Most soldiers are able to spot that, no matter how it's played."

"Yes, Sergeant." Peter put his trumpet to his lips and blew one raucous note. Both horses jumped and snorted.

Smith grinned and remarked, "As Job once observed of the war horse, 'Neither believeth he that *it is* the sound of the trumpet.' Try again."

Peter filled his lungs and blew a mighty but utterly anonymous blast.

"At last," said Sam Smith, "I can understand how it happened that day when Joshua commanded his trumpets to sound off, and the walls of Jericho came tumbling down."

"Just a minute, Sergeant," Peter pleaded. "I'll get it this time."

He shut his eyes and blew again. Now the sounds could be identified as a call of some sort, but no one could have been quite sure whether it was *Mess Call* or the *Funeral March*.

When Peter finished and looked up, the First Sergeant had retired to a distance and was holding his ears. But the three animals—the two horses and the dog—were gathered in front of him. Justin was stretching his neck out toward him, a look of concern in his dark eyes for his master who was evidently in great pain. Big Bill had sat down on his haunches as if such trumpeting was more than he could take standing up. Old Taylor, his muzzle pointed toward the sky, was howling as if his heart would break.

III

It was long before Peter was able to master double-tonguing with its *tu-ku* and longer still before he could tackle *tu-tu-ku*, which is triple-tonguing, the summit of trumpet playing. It was long before he was allowed to blow any calls at all, except in practice. Mackenzie was particular about the trumpeting in the 4th.

At last came the day when Peter was passed as competent by Sergeant Wills, the Chief Trumpeter. Grown gray in the service, Wills was said to date back to the period when a chief trumpeter was called Trumpet-Major. He ordered Peter to have the troop tailor sew the trumpeter's two one-half-inch yellow stripes along the legs of his breeches, the hunting horn insignia on the arms of his blouse, and attach the cap ornament, which was a horn with a "K" for his troop within the instrument's loop.

Wills also related traditions of the ancient and honorable art of trumpeting—how the call *Retreat* had originated in a Thirteenth Century Crusade—how the melodious night call of *Tattoo* was first used in the Thirty Years' War as a signal to tavern keepers that it was time to pull their taps to and draw no more wine for roistering troopers.

Until the Civil War, Wills informed Peter, the first eight measures of *Tattoo* had been repeated later in the evening, a call ordering lights out in barracks or tents, known simply as *Taps*. Then a musical Union general named Dan Butterfield, bothered by confusion caused among bodies of troops camped close together with one outfit mistaking another's bugle or trumpet calls for its own, composed a distinctive call for his brigade and one for each of its regiments. By blowing the few bars of the new calls before the regular calls, the Butterfield buglers identified them as applying to their own people. And these calls rallied the brigade in battle.

One evening a new tune for *Taps* had come to the General. He summoned his brigade bugler to his tent and whistled the notes for him to learn. The first night the new call was sounded, buglers all along the line were attracted by the charm of its slow, sweet strains and picked it up. It spread rapidly through the Army and was made official. Like the British *Last Post,* it came to be played also at military funerals as a soldier's farewell.

Sergeant Wills said: "Shannon, you've done well. You've turned into a pretty fair windjammer. Tonight we'll play *Taps*—four trumpets. I'll bring Kay from Headquarters.

Tell Elliot I want him there. You and he will play the echo."

The Texas night was cool and still. A crescent moon rode high through the cloudless, starry skies. The four trumpeters met in front of the guardhouse and blew gently into their instruments, warming them, making soft, guttural sounds. Wills and Kay faced in toward the post; Elliot and Peter, back to back with them, outward.

The Chief Trumpeter looked at his watch and raised his trumpet to his lips, the other three following suit. The two first trumpets blew the first phrase in two-part harmony. Elliot and Peter repeated it, also in harmony, before its last note died. Faced away as they were and playing more softly, their tones seemed to echo the others. They sounded the lovely, poignant strains of the call once, then repeated them.

Lights winked out in the barracks windows. Even the soft sounds of the evening were hushed. Peter, thinking, "This is beauty, and I'm helping create it," put all his soul into his playing. And the trumpets, sounding as mellow and tender as violins in the vast openness of the surrounding prairie, sang:

Fades the light
Falls the night.
Moon and stars
In the sky shining bright.
Night is on.
Fare thee well
Till the dawn.

The last echo died away in a whisper. Peter slowly lowered his trumpet from his lips, like someone waking reluctantly from a happy dream. Behind him he heard a soft, little sigh and a girl's voice speaking.

"Oh, Peter. That was beautiful!"

He had not known that Sally Ann was back from a long visit he had heard she and her mother had been making North. Of course, he would not have seen her anyway, after that quarrel of theirs in the kitchen. He had been too busy even to think of her—except offhandedly now and then.

"Thanks," he acknowledged her compliment. "But I'll have to admit that three other trumpeters had a little something to do with it, too." He turned to wave toward Wills, Kay, and Elliot who, strangely, had vanished.

Sally Ann was saying again: "I never heard it played more wonderfully. You don't know what *Taps* means to an Army girl, Peter. I've heard it ever since I was a baby. Mother used to sing it to me as a lullaby. I don't ever want to live anywhere but on an Army post where I'll hear *Taps* played every night. You must have worked hard to learn so well. Oh, I knew which was your trumpet and you sounded just as good as the rest. You were playing the second in the echo."

"Right," Peter acknowledged, gratified. "Yes, I have been doing plenty of practicing."

The girl gazed off into the night. "Sometimes *Taps* is sad," she said. "You feel that it's saying farewell to all the good soldiers who are gone." On Sally Ann's eyelashes tears glistened in the moonlight but she winked them away. "But most times it isn't sad," she went on. "It's like—yes, it's like the voice of someone you love dearly saying good-night."

The boy and the girl stood looking into each other's eyes, the spell of the night and the music on them. Peter thought: Did she think that when I was playing—that it was "like the voice of someone you love dearly saying good-night?" His heart was beating fast.

"Oh!" Sally Ann suddenly exclaimed. The same thought had run through her mind and she was demanding of herself in burning embarrassment: How awful! He must think I meant him. And the trouble is I did! "Oh!" she cried again. "I didn't mean—"

She turned and ran. Then she stopped abruptly, ran back and thrust a paper package into Peter's hands. "For you," she said and dashed away.

For a moment Peter stood motionless, in a half-daze. Stirring, he became conscious of the token left him. Slowly, he unwrapped it.

Cookies!

12: THE TRAIL OF GRAPES

I

COLONEL, Brevet Major General Ranald S. Mackenzie sat down to write his report to the Adjutant General, Department of Texas. And Trumpeter Peter Shannon sat down to write a letter to his father. It was October, 1872.

"With the five cavalry companies, in all seven officers and two hundred and fifteen enlisted men, and Tonkawa scouts," began the 4th's commander, "the march was taken upon McClellan Creek" . . .

"Dear Pop: As an old cavalryman, you'll know how I

felt," began Peter. "We cornered the Comanches at last, and I was ordered to sound the *Charge*." . . .

The veteran leader used precise military language, while the young trooper's pen was dipped as deep in boyish enthusiasm as it was in ink. But the eyes of Mackenzie glowed as bright as Peter's while they wrote, remembering.

The command had marched out as it had for numerous extended scouts in the past. But, having established a supply camp, it had headed straight for the Staked Plain and toward the several Comanche villages reported there.

Peter felt the current of anticipation that flowed through the column, a strong, though unjustified, sense of certainty that this time the enemy would not escape. The black Morgan beneath him seemed to share it, too. What a splendid trumpeter's mount Justin made! He now knew the calls as well as his master. Plainly he understood that a smooth gait would help when calls were being blown, for if he were at a trot and out of ranks when Peter began to sound off, Justin would shift into his easy single-foot.

Now Peter was carrying his trumpet slung tight up against his right shoulder blade, copying Elliot. From now on no calls would be sounded until they went into action. They were approaching enemy country, and brazen notes carried far over the plains. Nor would they be allowed fires any longer, for fear of betrayal by their smoke.

On the morning they were cooking their last hot breakfast, Peter took his little sack of coffee beans out of his saddlebags and went in search of the grinder carried in the mess chest.

"Take care of them beans for yuh, son?" Sergeant Hanks offered, as he was passing. To Peter's amazement, he opened a slot in the stock of his Sharps carbine, poured the beans in, inserted a small handle in a socket and ground the beans handily into powder.

Hanks grinned broadly at Peter's gaping. "Some of us got these here contraptions fixed up back in the war," he related. "Frequent y' couldn't find a grinder. Me, I never did take to chawin' coffee beans. I drinks mine and shoots better with it in me.

"Hain't no better shootin' iron than this here one made by old Christian Sharps. Thet's how come they called a good shot a 'sharp-shooter'—'cause he used a Sharps—not jest 'cause he'd got a sharp eye."

First Sergeant Smith, who had walked up, said: "We had another name for 'em, for Sharps rifles, before the war. Out in Bloody Kansas the anti-slavery men bought a lot of 'em to use on 'converting' the pro-slavery people. A good deal of the money to buy the guns had been raised by Henry Ward Beecher, the famous preacher. It was his sister, you know—Harriet Beecher Stowe—that wrote *Uncle Tom's Cabin.* Never was much doubt where the Beecher family stood on the slavery question. So in Kansas, seeing that Sharps were spreading the Reverend Mr. B.'s gospel, they were called 'Beecher's Bibles.'"

That breakfast was the last real meal in many hours. On pushed the cavalry column. It struck McClellan's Creek, named for a young lieutenant, later the organizing genius and commanding general of the Army of the Potomac, who had run a survey here twenty years ago. After marching two miles down the creek, the cavalrymen beheld a tempting spectacle—a wild grape vineyard, vines loaded heavily with luscious, thick-clustered bunches. All along the column, mouths were watering. Major Lindsay cast a questioning glance toward the General.

"Let the men dismount and eat all they want," Mackenzie answered. "No telling when they'll eat again. Grapes are good for 'em. Shrink their stomachs."

Peter stuffed his mouth full of the tart but tasty fruit, while Justin eagerly nibbled vine leaves. The 4th feasted fast but not long. An officer walking through the vineyard had discovered a trail of grapes and grape skins leading on from the farther side. Knowing Indians to be inordinately fond of wild grapes, he ran back to report.

Fall in. Mount up. Forward, ho. The commands were brisk and sharp. Traces grew plainer. This trail might lead to an Indian village: one might be hidden yonder in that valley along the creek.

The 4th took up the trot. Three, four miles they covered at a steady, swinging gait. Along the column blue-clad arms were upflung. Halt. Close up.

Still some distance further on, but clear in the bright sunlight of early afternoon, a Comanche village—a big one—stood revealed. There must be two hundred and fifty lodges and more. In the foreground the Indians' pony herd was spread out, grazing. And as yet neither herdsman nor warriors moving among the lodges had seen the poised column of blue.

Mackenzie signaled. Gallop, ho!

II

Men flung suddenly into combat do not think; they simply react. When they go more gradually into battle, approaching it consciously, as the galloping squadrons of the 4th Cavalry now did, most men shrink back instinctively as from the edge of a precipice. But the shrinking is usually only inward. Souls recoil but bodies advance, driven relentlessly by the will, dreading the road ahead that may have death at the end of it, yet dreading worse a turning back to contempt and dishonor.

To conceal or suppress this inner struggle and turmoil, soldiers resort to various subterfuges or distractions. Some laugh and joke, and the more lusty the jest, the more effective. Some sing or hum a tune. Some—and these are invaluable to any outfit—clown for their comrades, diverting others' minds as well as their own from the impending ordeal. Almost all strive to keep their faces expressionless, masking their thoughts. Thus it was with the troopers pounding down on the still unsuspecting Comanche village. There were some minutes of galloping ahead. They had plenty of time—more than many of them wanted—to think.

Peter Shannon thought: I've been in action before and didn't disgrace myself. I can't flinch this time. You either get hit or you don't. The trick is not to think about yourself. . . . He bent over a little to pat Justin below the withers where the mighty foreleg muscles were flexing rhythmically. Did horses realize they were going into battle? They must, Peter assured himself. He reached back to loosen his trumpet sling, grasping the instrument in readiness.

In the mind of First Sergeant Smith was a scene seeming to him no less vivid for having occurred one hundred and fifty years ago. The ex-professor was picturing Gustavus Adolphus of Sweden kneeling in prayer with his whole army before a great battle—Lutzen, wasn't it? One of history's strikingly memorable moments. Prayer, Sam Smith was telling himself, had its points as a prelude to battle. His lips moved silently.

The right hand of Sergeant Pinchon hovered toward his sabre hilt. His eyes were bright but faraway. Those were not Comanches yonder they were riding down on, but Prussians, the Prussians who only so recently had overrun his beloved France. Pinchon was singing *Le Chant du Départ.*

La Patrie nous appelle.
Sachons vaincre ou sachons périr.
Un Français doit vivre pour elle,
*Pour elle un Français doit mourir. . . .**

Sergeant Hanks, riding with the rear set of fours, grinned over at Peter in the fileclosers. He looked utterly unconcerned. Old "Peruna" Simmons galloped with the rapt look of one who hopes to find a long-desired release. Corporal Rick rode with his head hunched down between his shoulders. But it was the bearing of Lance Elliot that really fixed Peter's attention.

Elliot, right hand grasping his trumpet, its bell resting on his thigh, rode to the left and rear of Captain Bone at the head of the troop. Like the esquire and herald of a knight plunging into the fray, thought Peter. Or more like one of the hard-fighting medieval minstrels, troubadours . . . like that Tallefer of whom his father had told him . . . Tallefer who led the mounted charge of the Norman knights at the Battle of Hastings, singing the Song of Roland as he rode, tossing his sword in the air and catching it until he was in among the enemy, then smiting and hewing till he fell. Such was Elliot, one of those living for and loving the thrill and fierce joy of battle.

But not an officer or trooper, whatever his apprehensions, whatever his sudden, brief yearning toward loved ones at home he might never see again, could escape the stirring of pulses which comes to cavalry galloping into action.

An Indian on a mule had seen them. He tore for the village, shouting a warning. Herders tried to rush the ponies into camp and mount the warriors, but it was evident they would be cut off by the converging cavalry.

* Our country calls us. We must know how to conquer or to perish. A Frenchman must live for his country, for her a Frenchman must die.

Over the thundering of hooves Peter half heard an order, confirmed by Captain Bone's arm signal. "Right front into line." Rear fours swung out in an oblique to the right, increased their pace, moved up out of column into line. Peter glimpsed Sergeant Hanks' grin, as the movement brought him up on the right of the troop in line. Then came the sound he had been long expecting: the high, clear notes of Sergeant Wills' trumpet sounding the *Charge*.

"Draw sabre!" That was the troop commander's shout. Blades rasped out of scabbards, flashed in the sun. Every troop horse quivered, knowing that sound. Only Elliot and Shannon had not drawn. Their polished trumpets, catching the sunlight too, were at their lips, and together they repeated the call Wills had sounded. Its stirring, staccato summons echoed across the prairie. Charge! its brazen tones commanded. Sabres swept outward, points thrust forward. Men yelled hoarsely, menacingly.

Peter, sword out now, was seized by a breathless exhilaration. Justin was surging forward, tugging at his reins, hard to hold. His rider felt the glorious, driving power under him. Peter did not realize it but he was muttering to himself verses from the Scriptures Sam Smith had taught him:

"Hast Thou given the horse his strength? Hast Thou clothed his neck in thunder? . . . He saith among the trumpets, Aha! and he smelleth the battle afar off, the thunder of the captains and the shouting."

III

Charging troops thundered down on the big village. From its lodges, rifle fire crackled. Whistling lead and singing arrows began to hum through the oncoming blue ranks. Comanche warriors, making a stand, redoubled their fire.

Something dragged Peter's gaze to the right of the line. Where the set of fours which had come up from the rear with Sergeant Hanks was riding, there suddenly were four empty saddles. Three of the fallen troopers were mortally wounded, two shot through the neck, one through the stomach. The fourth had an arrow through his thigh. Steadily, keeping perfect formation, their four riderless mounts galloped on.

Sergeant Hanks? Peter, a catch in his throat, looked again. The Tennessean was still there beside the guidon-bearer. Hanks had sheathed or thrown away his sabre. Reins on his horse's neck, his carbine was at his shoulder and he was sighting carefully. Plainly the fire that had killed one or more of his men had come from an Indian marksman yonder between two lodges ahead. He was whooping in triumph as he reloaded. Hanks shot once. The Comanche whirled, threw up his hands and collapsed into an inert heap. His sightless eyes stared up at Peter as the troop rode over him. Not a horse stepped on the body.

Fighting through the village tended to break up the troop's alignment, yet it was roughly maintained, and gaps were closed. The four riderless horses on the right of the line still dressed on Sergeant Hanks as if at drill, until an Indian bullet smashed a foreleg of one of them. Left behind, the poor animal hobbled desperately with all his might, striving to catch up. Peter, his heart torn with pity, wanted to end the wounded creature's misery.

There was no time for deeds of mercy. On beyond the village, near the banks of a pool, a score or so of Comanche braves had rallied. Captain Bone, Corporal-Trumpeter Elliot, Sergeant Pinchon, and several troopers spurred straight into them. A red circle closed around the Army blue.

Peter at charge sabre rode straight for the circle. Justin

Charging troops thundered down on the big village

hurtled forward at a headlong gallop.

In charging enemy cavalry, horsemen against horsemen, a cavalry mount approaching the shock of battle usually will lift his head and forefeet as if about to take a fence. When about to hit enemy infantry, he will often gallop straight into a man and bowl him over. Thus Justin did now, plunging into the red circle. He smashed into one Indian with his left shoulder, then struck a second. Peter thrust downward to the right at a yelping savage grasping for his reins. The blade, caught between the ribs of the falling body, was wrenched out of his hand. He drew and fired his revolver until its hammer clicked on empty cylinders.

Still senselessly snapping his Colt, Peter emerged from his red battle haze to stare about him. Indian dead lay around him. More had slid into the pool, crimsoning its water.

Captain Bone's voice broke into his consciousness. "Good work, Shannon. You came in handy, joining our little ruckus here. Sound *Recall* now. Elliot can't manage."

Obeying, Peter turned to stare at Elliot. His friend was holding a bloody handkerchief over his mouth. "Lance!" he cried in deep concern.

"It's not bad," the wounded man's muffled voice reassured him. "Tomahawk cut across my mouth. Reckon I'm done with horn-tooting, though."

Peter started to help dress the wound, but Elliot pushed him away. "Stay with the captain," he ordered. "You're troop trumpeter now."

IV

The 4th Cavalry's casualties were four killed and several wounded. At least twenty-four Indians had been killed, and there would be more bodies at the bottom of the deep pool and others carried off. Undoubtedly, many of the fugitive warriors were wounded. Some one hundred and thirty women and children had been taken prisoner. These hostages, taken back under guard to reservations, probably would act as a magnet drawing Comanche braves away from the warpath to join them. The wounded were carefully treated.

What might have happened had the situation been reversed? Peter reflected. What would have been the fate of —yes, of Sally Ann (might as well admit he was thinking especially of her) if the Comanches had taken her? He shoved a highly unpleasant certainty out of his mind.

Now the lodges were being burned, along with all the Indians' food supply and all but a few choice buffalo robes. The chief booty, the Comanches' herd of three thousand horses and mules, was assembled under guard on the prairie after the Tonkawa scouts, as a reward for their services, had been allowed to take their choice of the finest racing ponies.

But that night the Comanches returned. Yelling and shooting, they stampeded the herd and ran off all but fifty of the captured animals. Mounted again, the Comanches, those superb horsemen, once more were a formidable threat.

"That, I'll lay a wager, will be the last time that happens," First Sergeant Smith remarked next morning. "If I know General Mackenzie, we will never again try to hold a herd of captured ponies."

"Why, the General wouldn't turn 'em loose, would he?" Peter asked.

"Not he. He'll have every last one of them shot."

Peter gasped and flung a protecting arm around Justin's neck.

"Shoot horses!" he cried. "Horses that aren't sick and wounded and have to be destroyed? All those spirited mustangs and beautiful racing ponies? General Mac couldn't be cruel like that!"

"War is cruel," said the big, bearded man softly. "Nothing that gives the enemy strength can be spared. I learned that on Sherman's March to the Sea." Sam Smith's eyes were sad as he gazed into the distance.

"But horses—it's not their fault. We ride them into battle. They don't go of their own accord—because they like it."

"Who knows? It may be that they have the same perverse, the same persistent fondness for war which is—or ought to be—the despair of mankind. Remember the verses from the Book of Job I taught you? The ones about the war horse?

" '*The glory of his nostrils is terrible.*
He paweth in the valley, and rejoiceth in his strength.
He goeth on to meet the armed men.
He mocketh at fear and is not affrighted;
Neither turneth he back from the sword.
The quiver rattleth against him,
The glittering spear and the shield.
He swalloweth the ground with fierceness and rage . . .' "

Peter nodded soberly. He recalled how he had recited later lines from the same passage riding into battle and how this black war horse of his had snorted and smashed furiously into the Comanches. He rubbed Justin's poll, facing him. Dark, eloquent eyes gazed into his—eyes that almost spoke—eyes that seemed to be giving him some message now.

A slow grin spread over Peter's tanned face. "Sergeant,"

he said, "it's crazy but I'd swear this fellow's been remembering the fight yesterday, just as we've been, and that he's trying to tell me something. Know what I think he's trying to say?"

"What?"

" 'Licked 'em this time, didn't we?' "

13: TROOP "K" GIVES A HOP

I

TEXAS would equal any state in the Union, if only it had plenty of water and good society, an enthusiast had boasted to General Sherman, down to inspect the border posts.

"Well," the General of the Army drily replied, "that's about all they lack in Hell."

The 4th Cavalry, forced usually to resort to its own society while stationed in Texas, found its own company tolerably good. Between scouts and campaigns, it fought the inevitable monotony of garrison life with a variety of diversions. Sprees and perfervid gambling sessions were regular sequels to the muster every two months for pay. After Uncle Sam's meagre stipend had been drunk up and gambled away by some, sent home or salted away by others, calmer pastimes succeeded—minstrel shows and other theatricals, hops, hunting. Mackenzie was liberal with his allowances of passes for hunting trips. He was well aware that they improved marksmanship, scouting, and trailing and provided fresh meat for the larder, as well as serving as recreation.

Mackenzie himself was an enthusiastic Nimrod. At Fort Sill he had kept a pack of foxhounds and ridden to them with all the ceremony and decorum of the hunting field, though the usual quarry was no fox but a wildcat. The regiment liked to tell of the time when the hunt, after a long chase, had run down a semi-wild pig, and how mad the General had been. The General also had been extremely put out (the annoyance of a commanding officer is always highly amusing to the rank and file when it has no repercussions on them) on the occasion when he had run a coyote miles with his greyhounds on a hot day, and ridden up to find hounds and coyote cooling off in the same pool.

Another favorite regimental yarn was of Lieutenant Miller's wild turkey hunt. That officer, shooting a big gobbler, had bent down in the brush to retrieve it, but when he grasped the bird by the tail, he found its head clamped in the jaws of a mountain lion. Ensued a terrific tug-of-war.

It was the lion that finally gave up and let go. Then there was the tale of the time Sergeant Pinchon had gone buffalo hunting, armed only with his favorite weapon, the sabre. The fiery little Frenchman had delivered a doughty thrust at a young bull, but the animal, instead of succumbing had, to the Sergeant's intense discomfiture, simply snorted with indignation and run off with the sword sticking in its hump.

The primary objective of several hunting parties especially sent out by "K" Troop several days that fall was neither target practice nor recreation, though it furnished both. The troop desired to set a bountiful table for a social affair. It was giving a birthday party, a supper, and a hop, for its First Sergeant.

II

Troop "K" barracks had been cleaned out and decorated. Cooks and extra details of kitchen police were engaged in furious activity. Bustle and excitement reigned in the quarters of the married non-commissioned officers and the laundresses along Soapsuds Row.

An invitation to the party had been conveyed to the Commanding Officer and accepted with pleasure. The Adjutant, Major Lindsay, his wife, and daughter, also had been bidden, along with the Squadron Commander and his lady. These, with Captain Bone and Lieutenant Hatton, the troop officers, would be the only guests from Officers' Row, and they would stay only for supper. This was an enlisted men's party, and no officer would wish to cramp it for long by the constraint of his presence.

Shaven, shorn, and uniformed as if for a general inspection, "K" Troop assembled in the festooned room. Outside the barracks the regimental band rendered some of the less martial selections in its repertory. In swept the fair with their escorts. Ma Simmons with Persimmons, acting a little genial for his having prescribed a stiff dose of Peruna for himself in honor of the occasion. Other laundresses, most of them with non-com. husbands. Sergeant and Madame Pinchon, a tiny, twinkling Frenchwoman who might have caused considerable trouble in the regiment had it not been for her own discretion, and her spouse's formidable skill with the sabre. Corporal "Hay" Rick, with a dark, flamboyant girl from a neighboring ranch.

The guest of honor entered, beaming. Sam Smith's high character and fair play had made him popular, though a First Sergeant. This birthday party for him was no attempt to curry favor but a tribute testifying to the honest liking the men of the troop had for him, a liking undiminished by the fact that his duty often compelled him to drive them hard. They cheered him, and pushed up to shake his hand in congratulation on his birthday. Peter, thronging up with the rest, was happy in the pleasure of his idol.

"Attention!" somebody shouted. Every trooper stiffened. Mackenzie had entered with Mrs. Lindsay—he being a bachelor—on his arm. Major Lindsay, Sally Ann, and other guests followed. "At ease. Rest," the commanding officer ordered, a smile on his dour face. Troopers obediently strove to be at ease and restful as ordered, difficult as it was in that august presence.

Supper was served promptly. Peter and others detailed as waiters staggered in with steaming, savory, heaped-high platters. Smoked buffalo tongues. Huge wild turkeys. Venison, bear meat, quail, and plover—the hunting parties had done nobly. There was roast pig, too, and salmon salad, jellies, and coffee and rolls. To cap the climax, the rare and delectable treat of real mince pies would be forthcoming for dessert. Troop "K" and guests, limited often enough to

Army rations—and short ones at that—fell on the feast as if famished. Waiters rushed back for more roasts.

"Hi, soldier!"

Peter stopped at the end of the table he was hastily circling. Sally Ann, her mouth rather full, had hailed him, and he had to be polite.

He had dropped in to see her quite often since the last campaign—to tell her how Justin was, of course—but he had meant to avoid her assiduously at this party. Given a chance, the troop would tease him unmercifully. But now she had spoken to him and, since it couldn't be helped, Peter stiffly and distantly replied: "Good evening, Miss Lindsay."

The hussy smiled up at him. "Sort of formal, aren't you, Pete?" she observed—too loudly. "But do keep it up. I like it. First time in my life I ever was called Miss Lindsay."

She polished off a large slice of turkey, and spoke again, just as Peter was about to escape. "The troop's putting on a real spread, and I can't help eating like a horse."

"Sally Ann," Mrs. Lindsay reproved her. "Don't keep that young soldier standing there. Let him go get something to eat himself."

"I was just making my manners and telling him how delicious supper is," the girl explained.

"Too delicious for you, young lady, I'm afraid," Mrs. Lindsay remarked tartly.

Sally Ann gazed up at Peter and smiled impishly. "Mother means I'm getting to be a big girl now, and I'd better watch my figure. But I don't see anything wrong with it, do you, Pete?" With complacency she regarded her trim form, still girlish but just beginning to round into maturity. Then she looked appealingly at Peter for an answer.

Sally Ann's last remarks had fallen in the midst of a

momentary silence. General Mackenzie himself began to roar with laughter. The laughter rose higher. Even those who had not heard the words joined in the hilarity at the sight of Peter's crimsoning face. The roar almost raised the roof as he beat a rapid retreat.

III

A scant half hour after the ceremonious departure of the guests from Officers' Row, Sally Ann was back at "K" Troop's barracks. She peered in a window. Mess tables had been cleared away. Most of the regimental band had disappeared; a few of its members, no longer doubling in brass, had transformed themselves into dance music. Fiddlers three, a couple of guitarists, and a concertina player were tuning up. With delight Sally Ann saw that Lance Elliot was there with his banjo. She guessed he would act as caller for the square dances. As a caller, he had no superior. The scar from the Comanche tomahawk showed livid across his lips; he would blow a trumpet no more. But voice and banjo would not fail him.

Sally Ann surveyed herself a trifle guiltily. Pigtails had been unbraided, and wavy, brown hair was flowing free, except for a bright red bow at the back of her head. Her skirt was a good three inches longer, a retractable hem having been let down. But guiltiest was her downward glance at the neckline of her flounced red dress. It had not been possible to lower that line from its modest cut, but beneath it the dress was tightly stretched over what appeared to be a precociously ample bosom. Sally Ann had borrowed two of her father's handkerchiefs, balled them up and stuffed them inside her bodice.

A set had formed, and the music struck up *Arkansaw*

Traveler. Lance's clear, strong voice, pitched to harmonize with the music, gave first call:

"Honor yo' partner. Lady on the left. All join hands and circle to the left."

Troopers bobbed heads and ladies curtsied. Slippers tapped and black Hessian boots thumped the floor. A merry circle whirled around and around to the lively tune. Sally Ann heard a soldier standing against the wall close to the window singing words to it.

"Oh, his horse went dead, and his mule went lame,
And he lost six cows. What a measly shame!
Then a hurricane came on a summer's day
And blew the house where he lived away.

"An earthquake came when this was gone
And swallowed up the land that the house stood on.
Then the tax collector came around,
And charged him up with a hole in the ground."

Elliot called for a Grand Right and Left and Promenade.

"Balance home.
Attention all!
All Grand Right and Left
'Round the hall.
When you come to yo' partners,
Promenade all."

Laughing, the dancers flung themselves into the figure. They swung from hand to hand and promenaded, some of the couples cake-walking. The watching girl could stand it no longer. She ran around to the door of the barracks and burst in.

"Sally Ann!" Stern tones halted her. First Sergeant Smith stood in front of her, barring her way.

"Why . . . Good evening . . . Uncle Sam." She used her private term of endearment for him. "I just dropped in to—"

"I bet your mother doesn't know you were coming back."

"She does, too, Uncle Sam. She said I could come back and listen to the music and w—"

"And watch. But don't go near the dancing." Sam Smith grinned at her.

Sally Ann stamped a foot angrily; then kept on tapping it in time to the music. "Look here," she protested. "I'm not picketed on Officers' Row yet. I know very well that when I'm a young lady I'll have to stick to the stuffy old hops the officers give. Enlisted men's parties are much more fun. Let me dance, Uncle Sam," she wheedled.

The corners of Sergeant Smith's eyes crinkled. "I thought you'd grown up already, Sally Ann," he said. "But since you haven't, maybe it's all right for you to dance."

"Oh, Unc—"

"But first," he insisted, "I'm going to ask you to lend me a handkerchief—or even a couple of handkerchiefs."

Blushing brightly, the girl removed the false "fronts" and passed them over. The sergeant himself led her out for the next dance. Lance saw her and sang out, twanging his banjo:

"Chase dat 'possum, chase dat 'coon,
Chase dat purty gal 'round the room.
Swing grandmaw, swing grandpaw,
Swing dat gal from Arkansaw."

Sally Ann flung herself into the figures with abandon. Peter, dancing opposite Ma Simmons (he had figured this attention would be good for cookie handouts all winter), suddenly caught sight of the new arrival. He gasped, forgetting his resentment at the embarrassment she had caused him earlier in the evening. Gosh, the girl was pretty with her hair that way! And grown up! She came toward him now on the call: "Turn the opposite lady."

"Hi, Pete," she greeted again. "I'm sorry about that talking too much at supper."

"Never mind," he said. "Say, Sally Ann, you look—"

The dance parted them before he could finish, but she had seen in his eyes what he meant and she almost hid her scarlet cheeks against Sam Smith's blue blouse when she skipped back to him for the alamande. Lance was chanting now:

"As I was a-goin' down the road.
I met Miss 'Possum and I met Mister Toad,
And every time the toad would sing,
The 'possum cut the pigeon's wing."

Ringing above the music and stamping feet, his voice was heard calling for another figure: "Do-se-do. Four hands 'round. Turn yo' partner. Turn the opposite lady. Swing yo' partner with both hands."

Peter found himself dancing with Sally Ann. Sergeant Smith and Ma Simmons had slipped quietly away and sat down. The fiddles were setting an even more rollicking rhythm, switching to *Green Grow the Rushes, O* and then to *Step to the Music, Johnny*. And how they stepped! By this time only young couples had survived, with the exception of Sergeant and Madame Pinchon, whose Gallic grace was the envy of all. Matching them were Corporal Rick, lithe and dashing, as he swung the tawny beauty he partnered till her skirts swirled high. But most eyes were following Sally Ann and Peter, for there was youth and young love living one of those glorious moments which come only in the springtime of life.

> *"Boys, go a-runnin' to that pretty little maid.*
> *Swing her like you love her. Promenade!"*

Peter would always remember Sally Ann coming dancing toward him, her hands outstretched. He caught them in his and swung her, swung her just as that call of Lance's had told him to. They were breathless when the exhausted musicians came to a sudden stop.

They found themselves facing Rick and his partner. Rick swaggered toward them, his bold eyes sweeping over Sally Ann.

"Dawgone!" he exclaimed, admiration plain on his over-handsome face. "The little Lindsay girl is no more. Like your ma said at supper, you're a big girl now. Me, I've been missing somethin'." He leered down into her flushed face. "Take you to a dance next time myself," he invited. "What say, Sal me gal?" Before the girl could answer or draw back, he chucked her roughly under the chin.

While Sally Ann stood speechless, half-furious, half-frightened, Peter stepped in front of her. Without a word he brought the heel of his right palm up against Rick's chin, so that the Corporal bit his tongue painfully.

Rick snarled. His right hand whipped down to where his Colt usually swung. Not finding it there, he stood hesitant and indecisive.

The dark girl walked closer. "You asked for that, Hay," she told her partner. "What else could you expect from a man of spirit. Me, I like this soldier. Maybe he will take *me* to a dance sometime," she said, rolling her eyes at Peter.

The dark girl laughed. Rick angrily grasped her arm,

and the two slipped away, leaving the dance. He had realized that his action had attracted considerable unfavorable attention, and it was prudent to depart.

Peter put the unpleasantness behind him. In the back of his mind lingered the thought that there would have to be a reckoning with Rick. Well, let that come when it must. Now there was Sally Ann and music and dancing—balancing at the corners, sashaying, grand-rights-and-lefts, and promenades. How could anyone prefer such slow round dances as the waltz when square dances were such gay and gorgeous fun?

For the last half-hour of the party they all stopped dancing and sang together, Lance Elliot leading, and strumming ringing chords on his banjo. After a number of old favorites, he swept the strings and with a wink at the major's daughter began to sing:

"Of all the girls that are so smart
There's none like pretty Sally.
She is the darling of my heart,
And she lives down in our alley." . . .

The song had Peter gazing soulfully at Sally Ann, and Sally Ann lowering her lashes demurely, then raising them again for a glance out of the corners of her eyes, to see if Peter were still looking at her that way, until all the company, noticing this byplay, was nudging one another and smiling.

Too soon it was time for the party to break up. Peter offered his escort home to Sally Ann, and it was promptly accepted. He began to shake a little inside. Would he, he wondered fervently, have the nerve to kiss her good-night? He certainly knew he wanted to! But maybe he shouldn't think of it. She was just a child, wasn't she—or was she?

She was going on sixteen, and he was nearly eighteen now.

If *Taps* were blown just as they reached the Lindsay quarters, he and Sally Ann—and that was just about the time it would be sounded now—*Taps* that she'd said was "like the voice of someone you love dearly saying good-night"—well, he was just going to have to kiss her.

That problem was solved for him in advance, as such problems sometimes are. Hardly had the girl finished shyly accepting his offer of escort home when Peter heard Ma Simmons firmly announce:

"I'm coming, too. 'Tis old enough you are now for a chapyrone, Sally Ann."

14: THE COMANCHEROS

I

TRUMPETER SHANNON, on orders from the Stable Sergeant, was instructing a recruit in grooming a horse and enjoying it hugely for more reasons than one. His detail as instructor meant that he himself no longer was regarded as a rookie but as a trooper of some seasoning. And in the performance of duty Peter's own mount was being groomed for him, since Justin was being used for demonstration.

Vigorously, the recruit, a farm boy, plied currycomb and brush on the sleek flanks. "Put your back into it," Peter nevertheless sternly directed. "Don't get the idea that just because this is a black, you don't have to get the dust out of his hide."

The recruit, looking pained, seemed to be about to say something. With all the gruff authority of an old-timer, Peter cut him off. "I'll do the talking, you do the listening. Maybe you have taken care of horses before, but not in the Army. The Army's different, I'm telling you. An officer's likely to walk over here and he might be wearing white gloves and run 'em over this animal. If any dust shows up on 'em, it'll be too bad for you. Guess you never struck anything like that on the farm, did you?"

"No, sir," responded the rookie, brushing away with all his might.

"Don't say 'sir' except to a commissioned officer," his mentor instructed. "Now get in there with the brush between his jawbones and down under his fetlocks—there's where grooming gets scanted. Brush out his mane and tail. When you've finished that, fetch a bucket of water and sponge those four white stockings clean. Then dry 'em with a clean piece of sack."

Justin was taking obvious pleasure in these ministrations. Though he lacked the means of signifying it that Nature has given the dog and the cat—the wagging tail and the purr—he managed to convey his contentment by standing very still and seeming to nap on his feet. But suddenly he pricked up his ears. A horseman, the new guidon-bearer, was trotting past the picket line.

It was Lance Elliot, accustoming his mount to the unfurled guidon he was carrying. Peter reflected how ideal an assignment this was for the former trumpeter. More than ever he looked a knight—a "verray parfit, gentil knight."

Above him like a pennon flaunted the forked flag, "U.S." in white on its red half, "K" for the troop in red on its lower white half. Its ferrule rested in a socket attached to his right stirrup. His right hand grasped its lance, as the nine-foot staff was called, terminating in a spearhead gleaming in the sun. Elliot lifted the guidon and practiced dipping it in salute. In that attitude he could have served perfectly as a model for an artist painting a paladin, with lance couched, about to ride a course against an adversary in a tournament or charge the foe in some hard-fought fray.

"Crickey!" the recruit exclaimed admiringly. "Lookit there! Reckon they'd ever let me tote a flag like that?"

"That's a guidon," Peter snapped. "Call it that. Only the cloth part's a flag. I suppose you'd call what's kept in the C.O.'s quarters and carried on parade, flags, too. They aren't. They're the national and regimental standards. If we were an infantry outfit, they'd be colors."

"Crickey!" the recruit said dolefully. "Kinda confusin', ain't it?"

"Not at all. Get on with that grooming." The recruit resumed so strenuously that Justin snorted and sidled away. Peter spoke in a kindlier tone:

"Sure they might let you carry the guidon some day, if you soldier well and keep out of the guardhouse and take good care of your mount."

First Sergeant Smith, walking up, confirmed: "That's right, especially the last mentioned. Private Shannon, do you know the fifteen points of a good horse?"

"Why . . . why," the confused instructor hesitated. Was that in the manual? He couldn't remember to save him. He stalled. "Why, Sergeant, this horse has more—lots more—than fifteen good points."

Justin, Sam Smith could have sworn, looked gratified and flattered. The Top grinned and continued: "Well, Shannon, perhaps you can't be expected to know that answer. It was given a bit before your time. It was stated in the year 1496, by one, Wynkyn de Worde. Here it is." He drew out his well-worn notebook and read:

" 'A good horse sholde have three propytees of a man, three of a woman, three of a foxe, three of a haare, and three of an asse.

" 'Of a man. Bolde, prowde, hardye.

" 'Of a woman. Fayre-breasted, faire of heere, and easy to move.

" 'Of a foxe. A faire taylle, short eers, with a good trotte.

" 'Of a haare. A grate eye, a dry head, and well rennynge.

" 'Of an asse. A bygge chin, a flat legge, and good hoof.' "

Peter laughed and said: "That's Justin all over."

"Crickey!" again ejaculated the recruit, completely baffled.

"Attention!" called the First Sergeant.

Major Lindsay was striding up to them. Peter began shaking in his boots. Here, he thought, comes my girl's old man, prepared to state in no indefinite terms that a certain trooper has been hanging around his daughter too much and he's to keep away, even if General Mackenzie is a friend of his father's.

Major Lindsay ordered Smith: "Sergeant, dismiss that recruit. No, Shannon, you stay. You're concerned in this." Peter's stomach started turning somersaults. "It's about this mount of yours." Peter relaxed. "There's grave danger again that you may lose him." Peter gasped and grew tense. The Adjutant continued:

"It seems those Cheyenne raiders didn't finish off José Pieda Tafoya after all when they jumped his wagon train. The old scoundrel's alive and kicking and back in business as a Comanchero on a bigger scale than ever. But I'll wager he's not too busy to have an eye out for lost property. For instance, a certain Morgan horse—a black gelding."

Peter felt sick with anxiety. His arm protectingly encircled Justin's neck.

"Sir," he pleaded, "don't let him take my horse. I've heard about that Tafoya. I know what he'd do to Justin. He'd just about ride him to death and then turn him out on the range in winter to starve."

"The boy's right, sir," Sam Smith supported him. "If the Major permits it, we'll just spirit this horse off to some hiding place for a while."

"That would never do, Sergeant. In the first place, I think we'd be caught at it. And anyway, the risk can't be taken. The General wouldn't like it a little bit. The U.S. Army can't be put in any such compromising position."

Peter sank into deep despair. What could he do against official opposition? Well, for one thing, he could call on Sally Ann for help. There was nothing she wouldn't do for her beloved Justin. She might manage to change the Major's mind. He'd noticed that the girl had an undeniable talent for twisting her father around her little finger.

But if that resort failed? Then he'd take Justin and "go over the hill." He knew Mackenzie's orders in regard to deserters: bring 'em back, dead or alive. Even so, determined Peter, setting his teeth, he'd do it rather than let Justin be turned over to Tafoya.

Major Lindsay must have seen the suffering in his face. "Hold on there, young Shannon," he interposed. "I don't intend to have your grand little horse here led over to Tafoya's hangout and tied up on his line with the Army's apologies. Tafoya will have to come and get him, and I've got a hunch he never will, and this is why."

The Major lowered his voice. "Don't forget, I was present when a settler, California-bound, traded this horse to Tafoya. And Tafoya can't identify him positively now. Why! Because this Morgan has *four* white-stockinged feet, and when that horse-trader passed him over he only had *one*."

"I don't quite follow the Major," Sergeant Smith said, perplexed.

"There's a silly superstition about a horse with four white feet being no good or bad luck. That trader had dyed black three of Justin's white stockings. I found it out when I picked up one of his feet which was wet. But Tafoya got fooled by the trick. Yes, I know I recognized the Morgan here again when Shannon brought him off the plain. So may Tafoya. But he lost a horse with one white foot and he can't swear to the animal's having four. If he does, I'll perjure myself with pleasure. So sit tight."

"Thanks an awful lot, sir," said Peter, sighing in the vastness of his relief and patting Justin's neck affectionately.

Neither the Major nor Peter could know that in the midst of the Cheyenne raid the wounded and prostrate Tafoya had gazed upward to perceive plainly that *all* of the black horse's legs—the cheap dye washed out by the water of streams through which they had passed—were white.

II

The post trader's store was divided into three rooms. In the center was the sales-and-stock-room, and on either side club-rooms, one for officers, the other for enlisted men. Each boasted no more than a billiard table (the worse for long, hard wear), chairs, a few tattered and ancient newspapers and magazines. Yet, they were welcome gathering places for bored and lonely men. A game of billiards or cards, a drink or so for those who had the price or credit, a place to air grouches or spin yarns, escape from cheerless quarters and barracks—all these the rooms gave.

Peter Shannon, on duty as a mounted orderly, rode up to the post trader's, tied Justin to the hitching bar and knocked at the door of the officers' club. Told to enter, he stepped in, saluted Major Lindsay smartly and handed him a bulky document, sent down from Headquarters for the Adjutant's signature. The Major regarded it with dismay.

"Paperwork, the curse of the Army," he groaned to club-mates. "This survey on seven lost glass inkwells already has eighteen indorsements. Orderly, wait. I'll call you when this is ready to go back. Wait in the other club-room."

"Yes, sir." Peter saluted, faced about and stepped out to cross over. From a window of the enlisted men's club-room he noticed a stranger, a civilian, staring out at Justin but paid little attention except to observe, as he entered, that the curious one was a rancher who was drinking at a table with Corporal Rick. The latter hardly spared Peter a glance, so engrossed was he in the news the rancher was imparting in a low voice.

"Yessiree, José Pieda Tafoya is back in the trade again and doin' fine. Sure, he got shot and sculped by Cheyennes and he was pretty near corked, but he come out of it fin'ly. Yup, he's countin' on you again, Rick. Says your news of what's up around the post was always worth payin' for. If it hadn't been for you warnin' him, Mackenzie would've nabbed him long ago. José sent you this." The man covertly slipped Rick a small sack that clinked.

Thus, with paid spies and accomplices, the Comancheros operated. Their money bought soldiers in the various garrisons; at one post there was a captain in their pay. They could well afford to share some of their large profits. Their trade with the Comanches, Kiowas, and other tribes of the Southwest was flourishing. With their goods packed on burros or even in sizable wagon trains like Tafoya's, they visited hostile tribesmen off the reservations and sold them firearms, ammunition, knives, paint, beads, calico, and whiskey in gourds. In their barter they cheated the red man as much as they dared, giving them as little as possible for their buffalo hides and "jerky" (dried beef in hide sacks), and the horses, mules, and cattle driven off in raids on ranches and settlements. The Comancheros disposed of these stolen animals to other ranchers and townsmen who bought them at a bargain and asked no questions.

The private conversation between the rancher and Rick was conveniently covered by noise made by a group at the bar. There Private Simmons was holding forth. A recruit had been treating the old soldier to whiskey, and he had consumed considerable. He was weaving back and forth and talking loudly and steadily, but every syllable was clear and not so much as a single sibilant slipped.

"There we were, standing general inspection," Peter heard Persimmons narrate to an interested circle. "The word had been passed that any trooper not perfect would spend the next two months doing extra fatigue. Along came the inspecting officer, known throughout the Service as 'Old Gimlet Eye.' Not a thing could he find wrong as he walked along the front of our rank. Sorely disappointed, he circled and snooped to our rear. Now it chanced that I had neglected to polish my spurs thoroughly. Of course Old Gimlet Eye spotted it. Breathing triumphantly down my neck, he barked: 'Trooper, are you aware that your spurs are rusty in back?' Never moving a muscle and staring straight to the front, I replied: 'No, sir. A good soldier never looks behind.' And the old boy never turned me in!"

Amid laughter, Persimmons poured himself another drink. "A further amusing anecdote comes to mind, if you would care to hear it," he continued. "At one time there was in my outfit a troop clerk with a talent for verse. Once, when I was compelled to go on sick report—something I ate had not agreed with me—this clerk set down the following poem after my name in the sick book:

"'Persimmons' soul on heavenly wings
Essayed to reach the skies.
The devil and whiskey held it down,
But the angels let it rise.
They could not lay embargo
Pure spirits in disguise.'"

Persimmons, leading the laughter, began now to drink from the bottle. His auditors looked uneasily at him, but no one did anything. It was Peter who strode over and took the bottle away. Firmly he pushed the old man outdoors.

"You're drunk, my friend," he said. "Get on back to barracks and sleep it off. You won't be able to walk past the sentry without getting thrown in the guardhouse. But you can ride. Get on my horse here."

"Thanks," Persimmons said thickly.

Peter untied the tie-rope. "Justin," he ordered, "take him back to the stables."

Obediently, the horse moved off at a steady walk.

The incident had again attracted the attention of the rancher to Justin. "Say, that might be the horse," he declared.

"What horse?" Rick asked carelessly.

"Tafoya lost a horse like that. A black with white feet. A Morgan, too." "Bah!" Rick scoffed. "We got a dozen like him in the troop—blacks with white markings, and . . . Wait! That nag *was* brought in off the Staked Plain by—. Look here, tell me about Tafoya's losin' a hoss."

For five minutes they talked excitedly in low tones. Then Rick stood up and smiled with malevolent satisfaction.

"That," he announced, "is something I'm right glad to know about. That hoss belongs to that young rat Shannon and he's dippy over it. Now I've got something that's really goin' to hit him where he lives!"

15: RIDE A COCK-HORSE

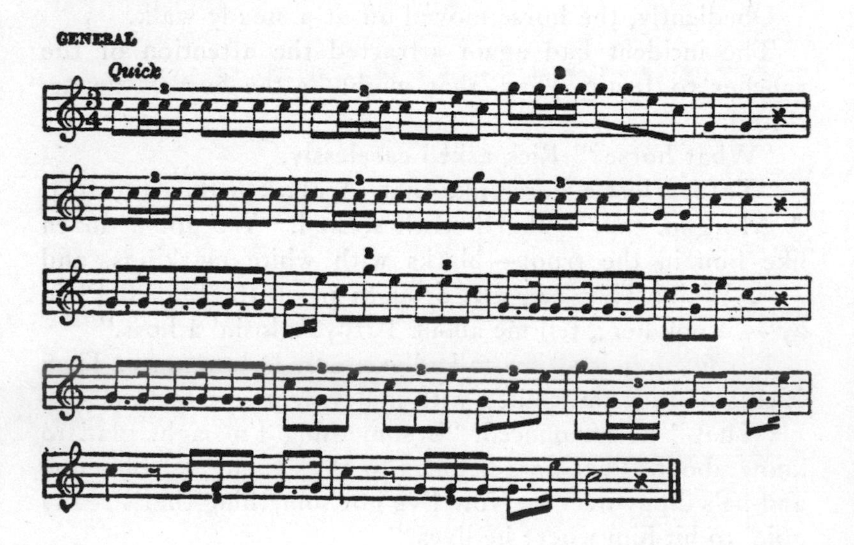

I

BETWEEN Justin and Old Taylor, the guardhouse dog, there had sprung up one of those strong horse-and-dog friendships sometimes seen. Except for the Morgan, Old Taylor's attentions were centered on prisoners and others in special need of comfort and companionship. Frequently, the part-bloodhound would trot up wagging his tail to pay a call on the horse, and as Justin lowered his head, the two would touch noses in a comradely fashion. Then they would pass the time of day together, and no witness would deny that they were holding a conversation.

Such a visit, being paid early one morning by Old Taylor, was interrupted by a trumpet call. Justin's ears pricked up and he tugged at the lariat picketing him. The hound barked. Both recognized the *General,* the call signaling march order. It carried through the bivouac, trumpet after trumpet echoing it, the notes of one overlapping another's—like singing a round, thought Trumpeter Shannon, sounding the long, difficult call for Troop "K."

March order was being signaled every morning now, for the 4th Cavalry was changing station. No outfit on the frontier ever was allowed to take root. There were frequent shifts to protect the vast territory under the Army's care, as parties of Comanches and Kiowas went on the warpath and Kickapoos and Lippans raided across the border from Mexican hideouts. Except for a few troops on detached service, the whole regiment was being moved, "horse, foot, and dragoons," as the saying went. The main body, now on the march, would be followed by a detachment convoying wives and children of Officers and Soapsuds Rows, the regimental band, and severely restricted baggage.

The good-bys said were not expected to be for long.

When Peter dropped in at the Lindsay quarters to say his, Sally Ann had told him:

"We'll be joining you soon at Fort Clark or Griffin or wherever the regiment's being sent. My, but I hate to leave here. Just as you begin to get sort of fond of a post, you have to pull up stakes and move out. I've had lots of fun here—like that last hop of your troop's. But orders are orders, and off we go. A change of station is generally for the worse. Prob'ly we'll have to live in a tent. At best, it means an old set of quarters with a new set of fleas and bedbugs. But such is life in the Army. Take good care of Justin, Pete. See you soon. 'By."

She had been as cool and matter-of-fact as that. It was true that the omnipresent chaperon, Ma Simmons, had been sitting there, but Sally Ann might have managed something warmer by way of a soldier's farewell. How did she know she was going to see him so soon—that nothing was going to happen to him? Lines from the *Faust* soldier's chorus ran through Peter's head:

> *And yet whate'er befalls us,*
> *We know that duty calls us.*
> *Farewell, farewell, my own true love. . . .*

He reflected somewhat bitterly on his discovery that the older girls grew, the more annoyingly impersonal they were apt to act.

No trumpeter should indulge in a train of disturbing reflections while he is sounding so intricate a call as the *General.* Peter made musical hash of its last few bars. Old Taylor howled reproachfully, Justin looked pained, and the First Sergeant shouted a stern reprimand. All of which was richly deserved.

Efficiently the veteran 4th put itself into march order and moved off. And then it rained.

It rained as if a billion buckets were being emptied from the sky. The trail soon turned into a canal of mud—mud which grew thicker and more clinging by the moment. Troop horses picked their way through it, but the wheels of the wagon train could not long escape its clutch. Down bogged the leading vehicle. Two troops were dismounted, grumbling and groaning under their breath. They made fast and stretched two long picket lines. The teamster yelled and cracked his whip over his team of six sturdy Army mules. The troopers on the lines heaved and cheered. Slowly, the wagon was pulled out of the morass onto firmer ground.

One after another, all the wagons of the train took their turn at bogging. Again and again, the weary tug-o'-war troopers had to help haul out vehicles hub-deep in mud. Every day it rained, and one day the struggling column made only three-quarters of a mile. Mackenzie, never a patient man, was furious at the delay. Yet he could not deny that his regiment was doing its utmost. Its veterans, mud-bound often enough in the Wilderness and other Civil War campaigns, used all the skills and tricks in their repertory. Officers and non-coms never hesitated to dismount in oozing sloughs and put their weight on wheels or ropes alongside enlisted men. Peter noticed only one exception. Corporal Rick took every possible advantage of his two stripes, directing busily but never lending a hand where it could be avoided. The trumpeter smothered his indignation; he could say nothing.

And still it rained. Uniforms and blankets were never dry. Every man and every article of equipment, excepting carefully-protected firearms, was covered with mud. They ate and slept in sticky slime. Trails turned into canals after the first few vehicles of the train traversed them. All the prairie seemed a veritable black sea of mud.

First Sergeant Smith stood beside Trumpeter Shannon while the latter, wet and miserable, blew a *Reveille* whose very notes seemed to shake and shiver.

"God made mud to discourage man from liking war too well," he said. "There's nothing glorious about it when you're marching as to war through mud like this. Unfortunately man will quickly forget the hardships and horror of warfare and remember only its stirring moments. Sound off again, Trumpeter, while I rout these poor devils of soldiers out of their blankets."

Now came snow and freezing weather to heighten the ordeal. Wagons froze fast in the quagmires and had to be dug out. Mules, striving mightily, slipped and fell. Now and then were heard revolver shots—a poor beast, with broken leg, being destroyed.

Peter, helping wherever he could, suddenly was struck with an inspiration. He went to Quartermaster Sergeant Connors and begged for a breast-strap and a pair of traces.

"For what would yez be nading the likes iv these?" Connors demanded.

"I'm going to see a fine lady from Banbury Cross," Peter explained with a grin. "You know, Sergeant. The lady who had rings on her fingers and bells on her toes and music wherever she went."

Connor shook his head sadly. "Sure, and I've seen it happen before with trumpeters. 'Tis no gun but only a horn they use, but they blow their brains out."

"No, I'm not crazy. I'm going to ride a cock-horse."

"A cock-horse, is it? Wait here, me lad, and rist. The march has been too hard on yez. I'll bring the surgeon."

"Aw, come on, Sergeant. Don't you remember your Mother Goose?"

"Me what! Me mither was no—"

"No, no. I mean the nursery rhyme." Peter hurriedly recited:

> *"Ride a cock-horse to Banbury Cross,*
> *To see a fine lady ride on a white hoss,*
> *Rings on her fingers and bells on her toes,*
> *She shall have music wherever she goes."*

With a look of decided alarm, Sergeant Connors hurried off in search of the surgeon.

Peter, helping himself to the harness, remembered that he had been as ignorant on the subject as Connors until his father had informed him that a cock-horse was a single leader hitched in front of a team in stagecoach days to manage a steep hill climb or a pull out of mud like the present.

Justin, breast-strap adjusted on him, seemed to know what was expected of him. Hitched on in front of a mule team, which had been unable to move their badly mired wagon, the black threw his strong chest against the strap. He plunged forward with all the drive of his sturdy legs, straining forward close to the ground. Pulling with skill and all his strength and weight, he tipped the scale for the struggling team. Out from the sucking mud lurched the wagon.

Justin, his white stockings vanished, his hide blacker still with black mud, looked up to receive his master's delighted approval. He also won another's. Major Lindsay had ridden up and observed his success.

"Fine work!" the Adjutant called. "Shannon, if there ever was any doubt about the amount of Morgan blood in that horse of yours, he's ended it now. He takes after his forefather for sure. The original Justin Morgan could haul heavier logs than any horse in Vermont. His master used to win many a gallon of rum betting on that—and couldn't I use some right now, hot and buttered! Bring your horse along after me. The General's trying to get a wagon unstuck up ahead, and I want him to see how it's done."

En route they were halted by the anxious Sergeant Connors, accompanied by the Surgeon.

"There he is, the poor b'y," the Sergeant called. "'Tis clane out iv his head he is. See for yourself, sor. He's not ridin' but drivin' his horse and there's no wagon behint. Kapes sayin', he does, he's to ride a cock-horse, whativer that may be. Some crature iv his dee-li-i-um, like as not, part-horse and part-rooster."

"Look here, Sergeant," Peter protested, "I—"

Connors broke in. "Nor is that the worse iv it. The poor b'y says he's bound for some crossroads to see a foine lady ride on a white horse. He might be m'anin' the Major's daughter."

Peter, blushing hotly, again vainly attempted to speak. So did Major Lindsay, looking puzzled and disconcerted. But Sergeant Connors was allowing no interruption.

"'Tis true Miss Sally Ann rides a white horse. And savin' the Major's prisince, 'tis up to tricks she is at toimes. But nivver have I seen her, like the b'y here sez, with bells on her toes!"

Peter managed a hurried explanation. Major Lindsay burst out laughing and ordered:

"That's enough, Sergeant. I know what Shannon's doing. Thanks, Doctor, but you're not needed. Trumpeter, come on—you and your cock-horse."

II

When they found Mackenzie, he had managed to extricate the first mired wagon and was on his way toward a second stalled one. Much pleased with Peter's scheme, he told him to follow with Justin.

The second wagon had not only been stopped by the mud but had several cracked wheel spokes. The cold and weary teamster was struggling to make some spot repairs with wire. Corporal Rick was indolently watching him, leaning on his mount's saddle. He failed to notice the two officers and Peter approaching on the other side of the wagon. As they came up, they heard him snap at the teamster to get a move on—heard the mule-skinner ask for some help—heard Rick sarcastically refuse him.

The mule-skinner, who had opened his mouth to hurl a few sizzling epithets, shut it abruptly. He saw his antagonist suddenly confronted by the enraged Commanding Officer.

Rick tried to manage the impossible feat of simultaneously jumping to attention while cringing like a guilty cur.

"Sir, I—" he faltered. His voice trailed off, as he stared aghast at the glowering fury in Mackenzie's face. Unable to meet the General's glare, he dropped his eyes. Perceptibly, he began to shake in his boots.

Mackenzie did not swear, but there was thunder in his tones when he spoke.

"Take those chevrons off your arm! I'll make a man of you!"

It took years to win non-commissioned rank in the old Army. Rick had been proud of his. His face worked as he ripped the stripes from his sleeves.

"Now get down in the mud and wire those wheels," the

General ordered. "Shannon, hitch your horse on. Teamster, get up on your seat and take the reins."

Spokes bound up, Justin and the team pulling hard, the wagon emerged handsomely from the mud.

Peter, moving on, caught only the last of the words Rick muttered as he passed back of him.

"— you, Shannon! You brought Mackenzie 'round. You got me busted. I'll fix you plenty!"

III

The 4th reached the Red River at last, but it was full to its bank, the current rapid. One old scow, the only means of ferrying over personnel and baggage, plied back and forth. Unless a further long delay was to be suffered, the horses must be swum across. Mackenzie gave the order. "Have the best horsemen and swimmers lead off. Round up the rest of the animals and drive 'em in riderless, right after the leaders."

Peter was proud when he and Justin were among those selected to lead the way. Ridden to the bank, the black Morgan was plainly reluctant and nervous as he looked down into the rushing water, yet he responded to gentle urging and his master's will. In he plunged, snorting. Peter clung to the mane on the outstretched neck. Icy water gripped his thighs, as Justin swam across steadily and scrambled up on the opposite bank.

The unridden horses had seemed to understand and be willing, but they had hardly entered the river when panic seized them. They wheeled, rushed back for the shore and stampeded, knocked down and trampled their herders. They ran miles before they were caught and returned. It was three days before they were all ferried over.

Yet, once across the river and free of rain and mud, the long march settled to steady and comparatively easy progress. There was hot food again and campfires and grazing for the horses. Men sat around the fires luxuriating in dry clothes. Life, no longer seen through a dismal downpour or drizzle, looked brighter, and they could laugh at incidents of the march which never had drawn even a chuckle when mud was squelching in over boot tops. There was, for instance, the recently joined young officer who had mixed up his commands ridiculously. Recounting it, Sergeant Hanks added the tale of the green colonel of Volunteers in the Civil War who carried in one hand slips of paper on which were written the commands for drilling his regiment. All went well until his horse shied and he dropped the slips. Then he had to order the regiment dismissed. Hanks told also of another officer who, not knowing how to march his company over a ditch, extemporized the original command: "For that ditch, look out!"

First Sergeant Smith followed with more yarns of the war. "There was, believe me or not," he said, "a regiment organized in Iowa that was made up entirely of temperance advocates. There was a husky Pennsylvania company whose personnel was all blacksmiths. But the idea that always appealed to me most was the proposal of a fellow named Smith that he recruit a whole regiment of Smiths. Its roll call would have been worth hearing."

Peter, with deference to the old-timers, ventured to contribute some lines from a letter an uneducated recruit had asked him to write home for him: "Down here there's wild beasts, captains, centipedes, lieutenants, tarantulas, sergeants, corporals, and rattlesnakes."

Sam Smith, pulling out the well-worn notebook, read an epitaph copied from a lonely grave along a prairie trail:

"here lies the body of Jeems Hambrick
who was accidently shot
on the banks of the pecus river
by a young man
he was accidently shot with one of the large
colt's revolvers with no stopper for the cock to
rest on it was one of the old fashion kind
brass mounted and of such is the kingdom of heaven."

"Most cavalrymen like a horse story," Lance Elliot put in, "and this is one of the strangest and most striking ones I ever heard. Happened down where it looks like we might be heading—in Mexico. When Cortez and his Spaniards invaded in Fifteen-Hundred-and-Something, it was their war horses that won many a battle for them. The Aztecs and the other Indian tribes were scared to death of the horses. They'd never seen one before—thought they were gods.

"Cortez rode a magnificent, big black named El Morzillo. But the charger went lame—picked up a splinter in his forefoot. Cortez had to leave him in charge of an Indian chieftain. 'See you take the best of care of him,' the Conquistador growled through his bristling, black beard. 'If I find you have not done so when I return—if my beloved steed is not here where I left him—.' Cortez did not have to go into details on what would happen. The Aztecs had seen plenty of evidences of the wrath of the Conquistadores.

"But Cortez never did return. Neither did any other Spaniard come that way for more than one hundred years. Then two Franciscan friars happened by. On an island in the middle of a lake they found a temple and in it was the statue of a horse, carved out of stone, sitting on his hindquarters just like the Top Sergeant's horse, Big Bill. The Indians were worshipping the image as the God of Thunder and Lightning.

"Yes, it was a statue of El Morzillo. This is what had happened. The Indians had stabled the horse in the temple, where the best of care could be taken of him. Maidens hung garlands of flowers around his neck and offered him fruit, chickens, and all sorts of fancy food. Well, the black charger died—whether from not getting proper forage or from old age, nobody knows. The Indians, stricken with terror that Cortez would return and take some terrible revenge when he found his horse gone, carved and set up a statue of El Morzillo in the dead animal's place.

"If it still were there it would be worth a long trip to see. I declare, I always thought there were too many statues of men and not enough of horses. But because the stone horse was being worshipped by the Indians, the monks cast it down as an idol and shattered it."

Peter, wrapped up in his blankets beside the campfire embers, slept and dreamed. It was a jumbled dream in which the Conquistadores, King Arthur's Knights, and the U. S. Cavalry were fearfully and wonderfully mingled. Peter saw himself being rowed toward an island in a lake by Indians who must be Aztecs, though they looked like Comanches. He sprang from the boat and strode toward a temple, his sabre clanking at his side. He wore steel helmet, breastplate and, surprisingly, a beard as heavy and black as that of Cortez. He *would* have to start shaving now—or would he?

Within the temple stood a splendid, black steed. Peter recognized him with joy as Justin. Maidens had groomed him so beautifully that no inspector, no matter how crusty, could have found fault, but they were busy now hanging garlands of flowers all over him. That, of course, was not according to Army regulations, and Peter was about to object when the chief maiden came forward.

Oddly, she didn't look at all Indian. She had wavy, brown hair, tied in the back with a bright red bow, laughing brown eyes, and a saucy smile. In fact, she looked exactly like Sally Ann.

"Fair maiden," Peter addressed her, "a thousand thanks for your care of this, my favorite charger."

The maiden bobbed him a curtsey, which wasn't very Indian either, but which was most fetching and replied:

"Kind Sir, it was both my privilege and pleasure to care for this goodly steed of yours. Within my heart"—she placed her hands over it in an appealing gesture—"has sprung up for him such devotion as only his master could surpass."

"He *is* a grand horse," Peter acknowledged, "but nonetheless I must reward you for your care of him. What guerdon would you prefer? A necklace of rubies, or a bracelet of virgin gold, thickly encrusted with emeralds?"

The maiden shook her head and cast down her eyes demurely. Apparently she didn't care for jewelry, or maybe her mother wouldn't let her accept such presents from men.

Peter, completely at a loss, stood racking his brain. At that moment Justin gently shook off three maidens and five or six garlands, walked over and whispered in his master's ear.

Listening, Peter blushed right through his beard. "Thanks, Justin," he said. "That *is* an idea for a reward."

He strode over to the maiden who, awaiting him, never stirred. She turned her face up toward his, closed her eyes, sighed in grateful and blissful anticipation and pursed her pert lips.

Peter was bending down graciously, even eagerly, when—

Someone was shaking his shoulder roughly. Peter woke to see Sergeant Pinchon bending over him in the half light. With a twinge of alarm he remembered that the sergeant had been in charge of the "K" Troop herd guard last night.

"Réveillez! Immédiatement!" Pinchon was saying urgently, so urgently that he had reverted to his native tongue. *"Hélas,* your horse he has disappear'!"

16: THE PRISONERS' FRIEND

I

STILL heavy with sleep, Peter could only keep repeating: "But how could he disappear? Justin never strays."

"No, nevaire," Sergeant Pinchon agreed. "I cannot understan'."

"Wait!" Peter was wide awake now. "Who was on your herd guard?"

"Why you ask? *Ça ne fait rien.* All old soldier—no recruit."

"Quick, Sergeant! Was Rick on it?"

"Le brigadier ci-devant? The busted one? But yes, Rick was of the guard. But—"

"That's it then. Rick's had it in for me. Thinks I got him busted. He drove off my horse to get even."

Peter could see it as plainly as if he had been an actual spectator. Rick circling the herd while his relief was on post—waiting till the other sentry and the sergeant were on the opposite side—pushing in among the black troop horses and cutting out the white-footed Justin—hazing him away when he tried to rejoin the other horses. Then, a vicious lick with a quirt or a knife jab in hindquarters, and the Morgan, hurt and startled, dashing off into the night.

Pinchon was protesting. "No, Rick he is no good, but that he would not do. I have question him. I—"

Peter cut in vehemently. "You don't know him. Lend me your mount, Sergeant. Justin can't have gone far."

"I have already made scarching, riding off from camp."

"Please, Sergeant, let me try. You know how I feel about that horse. I think I know how to trail him."

The Frenchman yielded, with the stipulation that Peter be back before the *General* was sounded. In a rush the trumpeter snatched up Justin's saddle blanket and rode his borrowed mount over to the prisoners' bivouac.

Sceptics always insisted it was a mere fluke, but, in the opinion of most of the regiment, Old Taylor that day proved that his bloodhound strain was authentic and talented. Peter, making him smell Justin's blanket, had persuaded the hound to leave the prisoners. Somehow they had struck a trail leading away from the place where the herd had grazed. Old Taylor followed its thread through other hoof-prints. Nose to the ground, he lumbered on, plainly having the time of his life. Never before had this instinct of his been so gratifyingly used. Even the stern Mackenzie had not been able to bring himself to order Old Taylor, the prisoners' friend, employed to catch a soldier escaped from confinement.

Peter, riding close behind the hound and as absorbed in the hunt, paid little more attention to where and how far they were going than did Old Taylor. They took no more than passing notice when the trail of Justin merged with that of several horses and that trail in turn into a herd's, interlined with wheel marks. Almost before they saw it, they had overtaken a wagon-train. A stout, gaudily-dressed horseman, backed by two tough-looking *vaqueros,* barred their path.

"Well, *Señor Soldado?*"

Peter recognized from descriptions that he was being addressed by José Pieda Tafoya himself. Here was the man who once had owned Justin—who must have won him back now, if the trail had not deceived. At a loss what to do, knowing only that he must somehow recover his horse, the trumpeter sat dumb on his borrowed mount.

Tafoya repeated his question, insolently, impatiently.

"Somebody ran off my horse," Peter finally brought out in answer.

"So? Would you accuse me?"

"I'm not accusing anybody—yet. But I'm going to get my horse back, no matter who's got him."

The Comanchero shrugged. "I am well accustomed to being accused by soldiers. What sort of a horse did you lose?"

"A Morgan gelding. Black with four white feet."

"So? Well, let your own eyes convince you, *Señor Soldado.* My herd yonder is a small one. In it are a few blacks, but none with white feet."

Peter would have ridden over toward the herd, a hundred yards or so off the trail, but the *vaqueros* did not seem disposed to move out of his way, and he could scan the horses from where he was. He picked out the blacks. One of them from a distance looked rather like Justin, but neither he nor the others had white feet.

Too distressed and excited to remember Major Lindsay's story of the black dye, Peter sat nonplussed. It failed to occur to him that Tafoya, having once been taken in by the blackening of white stockings, could turn the trick to his own advantage. Squirming under the trader's contemptuous smile, he turned his mount to leave.

But Old Taylor was not to be fooled by such surface trickery as dye. Suddenly he rushed over to the horse herd and leaped up clumsily to nose the muzzle of the black Peter had thought resembled Justin.

"There he is!" Peter shouted exultantly. "Now I know him. That's my horse."

"By your own words, *Señor Soldado,* you are mistaken," Tafoya remarked suavely. "You said he had white feet."

Peter spoke up hotly: "I see through your trick, Tafoya. That horse is mine. You've dyed his white stockings, but you won't have had time yet to burn over his 'U.S.' brand or his hoof-mark."

Now it was Tafoya's turn to fume in silence, unable to make an answer.

"Turn over that horse," Peter demanded. "If you don't, I'll report him stolen to General Mackenzie. He's not far off. I've got an idea you wouldn't care much about meeting him."

Obviously *Señor* Tafoya would not. He was so little eager to meet the General that he would not risk arguing his perfectly good claim to the Morgan horse.

Yet neither was he knuckling under to this youngster. His air of suavity slid way to unmask a menacing stare. He motioned, and his *vaqueros* rode over to Peter, shoving guns in his ribs, making him raise his hands. Somebody behind clubbed the trooper on the back of the head. He slumped in his saddle and toppled to the ground.

II

Old Taylor was serenely happy. When they whipped him away from Justin and ran him off from the wagon-train, he had been highly indignant; he was not used to such treatment. He had fled yelping. Then he had sat down at a safe distance and watched to see what happened at the train. How fortunate it was he had waited. Now he had a prisoner to befriend.

The prisoner lay bound and gagged in a small, brush-covered gulch. The hound had seen the wagon-train men hide him there and take their departure. Promptly Old Taylor had crawled in and joined the prisoner. It could not have been cozier.

This was altogether the most satisfactory prisoner Old Taylor ever had befriended. Old-timers in the guardhouse were apt to weary of his attentions. Sometimes they cuffed him away when he sought to comfort them in their confinement. This prisoner did not object even when his face was lovingly licked.

Old Taylor's ministrations finally brought Peter Shannon, heavily stunned by the blow on his head, back to consciousness. After a time he tried to work the gag out of his mouth and free his arms or legs. All his efforts were futile; the Comancheros had tied him up well. Old Taylor observed him sympathetically. The expression in his mournful eyes seemed to convey: "I know a prisoner's lot is a hard one. But be of good cheer. I'll stand by you."

And he did. He never moved when twice the rhythmic hoof-beat of 4th Cavalry patrols, searching for the missing trumpeter, passed close to the gulch. Peter glared wildly at the bloodhound. He grunted, groaned, and kicked at him with his trussed-up legs, doing everything possible to make the dog howl or flush himself from the gulch to reveal it to the patrols.

Maddeningly, Old Taylor refused to leave the spot. He stood fast, maintaining a dignified, I-know-better-than-you-do attitude. Often enough Old Taylor had seen guards come for prisoners, hale them away from snug repose in the guardhouse and work them hard all day in back-breaking fatigues. The prisoners returned tired and unhappy, and Old Taylor felt for them. Let this prisoner have a good rest.

Peter gave up. Worn out, he slept for a while, only to wake up and struggle hopelessly against his bonds. Leaden hours dragged by, and the dread of dying ingloriously, tied up in a hole in the prairie, loomed ever larger. It grew much colder as night fell. Peter moaned through chattering teeth.

Old Taylor, sensing suffering, saw an opportunity to be of service. Besides, he was growing chilly himself. He snuggled closely to the prisoner. But the dog's warm body did not prevent the chills which shook Peter's body, alternating with feverishness.

Next morning the hound, grown hungry, emerged from the burrow to hunt. In the pursuit of a jack rabbit, he sighted the 4th Cavalry's wagon-train. Barking, he led searchers to the gulch and the now delirious prisoner.

He slumped in his saddle and toppled to the ground

III

The 4th Cavalry had ridden back to station after an invasion of Mexico. Mackenzie had made a swift and effective raid to punish the Kickapoo and Lippan Indians whose depredations in the United States had gone unhindered by the Mexicans—had made it under only verbal orders from General Phil Sheridan, running grave risk—had made it brilliantly without losing a man. Troop "K's" trumpeter, who had fallen sick while the regiment was en route to Mexico and had been invalided back to the posts, could not be listed as a casualty of the raid.

It was before the day of the Army nurse. The little post hospital, where Peter lay making a fight for his life with pneumonia, furnished only such nursing care as overworked orderlies, Medical Corps men, could give. Mrs. Shannon had been telegraphed for, but it would require some days for her to arrive. Meanwhile, the constant attendance which the surgeon wanted Peter to have was supplied by men of his troop and the women of the garrison.

Sometimes it was big bearded Sam Smith who sat by the bed, his heart aching as he watched the boy struggle for breath. Sometimes it was Lance Elliot, deeply brooding, gentle and deft. The women of the post took regular turn: Mrs. Lindsay, Ma Simmons, Madame Pinchon. Nor could the youngest of them be kept away. But Sally Ann's mother would not let the girl's nursing tours last long or come frequently, despite her protests. Sally Ann, possessing the self-reliance Army girls soon learned, was a dependable and efficient nurse. But after two hours of watching Peter gasping and raving in delirium, she ran home to fling herself on her bed, racked by uncontrollable sobs that left her exhausted.

The surgeon, meeting Mrs. Lindsay just coming on duty to nurse Peter, told her: "I think the crisis will be today. Whether he gets past it or not is a toss-up."

"Doctor," Mrs. Lindsay ventured, "my young daughter has the idea this boy is badly worried about something. Is it possible that something on his mind could hinder his getting well?"

"Possible—yes. It may be his mother's absence. He keeps calling for her. Most of 'em do, at any age, when they're going out," the surgeon added sadly. "Mrs. Shannon is due tomorrow. I wish she could have made it today."

"Sally Ann is a flighty young thing at times and then again she knows what she's talking about," her mother conceded. "She insists the boy is worried about that horse of his he was looking for when he was knocked on the head."

"Oh, I doubt that," the surgeon deprecated. "Well, we'll hope for the best. Call me whenever I'm needed, please, ma'am."

Sally Ann thought: He doesn't know and he *has* to know. I can tell that from what he's said, even if he is out of his head. I've tried so hard to tell him and he can't seem to listen or understand.

Indeed she had tried hard to tell him. She had whispered to him often: "Peter, Justin's here. He's all right. We got him back. Our patrols picked him and Pinchon's mount up, loose on the prairie. The people that hit you must have turned the horses loose when troops got close to them. General Mac couldn't stop to follow it up—he was riding for Mexico. But we've got a good idea who it was. Anyway, Justin's back. That's the big thing. That's what you want to know. Justin's back. Pete dearest, can't you understand?"

But Peter couldn't. He stared off into space with eyes that saw nothing.

It was Sam Smith's tour by the bedside. He sat there, sorely distressed. The young fellow looked to be in bad shape.

The First Sergeant tried to draw a prayer for the sick out of the rich store of his memory but could remember none. Instead, inappropriate though it was, the former professor found himself repeating the tremendous adjuration from Ecclesiastes. There was such strength and majesty in the words. Softly, his voice deep and sonorous, he recited:

"Remember now thy Creator in the days of thy youth, while the evil days come not, nor the years draw nigh, when thou shalt say, I have no pleasure in them.

"While the sun, or the light, or the moon, or the stars, be not darkened, nor the clouds return after the rain:

"In the days when the keepers of the house shall tremble, and the strong men shall bow themselves, and the grinders cease because they are few, and those that look out of the windows be darkened,

"And the doors shall be shut in the streets, when the sound of the grinding is low, and he shall rise up at the voice of the bird, and all the daughters of musick shall be brought low:

"Also when they shall be afraid of that which is high, and fears shall be in the way, and the almond tree shall flourish, and the grasshopper shall be a burden, and desire shall fail: because man goeth to his long home. . . ."

Why, Sergeant Smith wondered, should he speak that passage in the presence of an unconscious, dying boy? Because one still in the days of his youth was coming, untimely, to the end of his span?

Sam Smith looked over to find Peter regarding him out of clear, lucid eyes. At that moment the window opposite the bed was flung open and in it appeared Sally Ann, pulling in beside her eager face the crested head of a black horse.

"Look, Pete," the girl called. "I told you we got him back!"

"Justin!" Peter cried, and in his voice was all the joy and relief for which anyone—even Sally Ann—could have hoped.

17: THE GIRL LEFT BEHIND

I

MOUNTED drill was being stepped up. In the 4th Cavalry that usually meant another campaign, or at least an extended scout. The drill ground echoed to trumpet signals and shouted commands. Form fours, trot, march. . . . By twos, trot, march—the "march" drawn out into the long, ringing "ho" of the mounted service.

Non-com instructors reeled off passages of the drill regulations. "At the command: Prepare to fight on foot, all dismount except Number 4 to whom the others pass their reins. Numbers 1, 2, and 3, having linked horses by tying reins to cheek-pieces and nosebands of the halters and bridles of the next horses, they face front and hook up their sabres." Distraught recruits strove to obey, only to be barked at: "Naw! Not that way. That's no good. You act like you got paws. Them's hands on the end of your arms, rookie. Hey, there! Don't you savvy English? 'As you were' means as you was before the last command was give. C'mon now!"

Trumpeter Shannon, back on duty after a long convalescence furlough, enjoyed it all to the utmost, more especially because he probably would not have many more months with the regiment. His father had refused to allow him to re-enlist, insisting that it was time he went to college. The studying he had done under the able tutelage of First Sergeant Smith was highly commendable; it probably would enable him to pass college entrance examinations. As for Peter's plea that he be allowed to stay in the Army and perhaps win a commission from the ranks some day, John Shannon turned that down firmly. Peter put aside the hope for the time being and followed the advice of the old Roman to whose works Sam Smith had introduced him: the sprightly poet Horace, who counseled, *Carpe diem.*

Galloping Justin after the troop commander, sounding calls clearly and rapidly, Peter envied no man. It seemed to him that there was no detail in the cavalry as dashing as trumpeter, unless perhaps it was carrying the guidon. But he held no envy, only admiration for his friend Lance Elliot, racing across the troop front when the guide changed, his guidon flaunting like a gonfalon.

The cavalry! There was no arm in the service to match it. Peter was steeped in its lore by his father's stories, by Smith's and Elliot's, by his own reading of the exploits of cavalry in the Napoleonic and the recent Franco-Prussian wars. If he half-closed his eyes, Troop "A" yonder became hussars, jaunty jackets called dolmans swinging from left shoulders. Troop "C" turned into dragoons, originally so-called because of their short carbines with muzzles shaped like the head of a fire-spouting dragon. "E" Troop over there, its mounts larger than average, could be cuirassiers—heavy cavalry which had taken their name from the leather breastplates they wore when first organized. With their chest armor and crested helmets, cuirassiers closely resembled ancient Greek warriors. Peter's own troop was transformed by his lively fancy into gallant lancers, wearing the square-topped Polish caps which always distinguished that type of cavalry and carrying pennoned lances. No great stretch of the imagination was required for that transformation. There had been lancers in the U. S. Army as late as the Civil War, and there were crack lancer regiments in the European armies today, notably the German Uhlans and the Russian Cossacks.

Come to think of it, Peter mused, the 4th Cavalry was now about to take the field against formidable lancers, the Comanches. A mounted charge by those fierce tribesmen, their lances tipped with captured bayonets or pieces of sabre blade, was something you didn't care to face twice, veterans admitted.

Early one afternoon drill was replaced by issuance of ammunition and field rations. To Peter it was plain enough he would be blowing *Boots and Saddles* next morning for the regiment to march.

He was mistaken. Orders came to sound the call later that same afternoon. General Mackenzie's impatient temperament seldom brooked any avoidable delay.

II

The 4th Cavalry's fine band was formed in the center of the parade ground. At most frontier posts it had become a cherished tradition to "play away" an outfit marching off on a campaign which might well last a long time and take a toll of casualties. Whether the music was simply fifes and drums or a full brass band, the tune always played was *The Girl I Left Behind Me.*

Peter had ridden off to that lively air before, but today it seemed for the first time to hold deep and personal meaning for him. Since his return, Sally Ann had been shy, which wasn't at all like her but had made her more alluring than ever. He had tried to tell her what her bringing Justin to the hospital window that day had meant to him. She had insisted on passing it off. "It was a crazy trick," she said. "Believe me, I caught it from the family for doing that!" When he vehemently protested that the sight of her and Justin, framed in the window, was the remedy that really made him well, she had only smiled mysteriously. Peter was certain that girls stood before the mirror for hours practicing smiling mysteriously. Anyway, they managed it, although how they did was a mystery—and an annoying one—to him.

Troops formed in their areas and moved into column of fours. Disappointment gripped Peter more bitterly. This early departure had given him no chance to say good-by to Sally Ann. Even a very proper and formal farewell would have been better than none at all.

Now the band was striking up the traditional tune. Its words ran through Peter's head.

I'm lonesome since I crossed the hill,
And o'er the moor and valley.
Such heavy thoughts my heart do fill,
Since parting with my Sally.

"Sally." It was almost too pat the way songs kept bringing in that girl's name. Probably it was just for a rhyme. Sally . . . valley . . . alley. But it *was* kind of a nice name.

Bay and sorrel and chestnut troops were turning into the regimental column. The blacks of "K" stamped restively.

Oh, ne'er shall I forget that night.
The stars were bright above me
And gently lent their silvery light,
When first she vowed she loved me.

Of course she never did vow she loved me, thought Peter. But what she said and the way she acted that night we blew *Taps* in four-part harmony got me feeling she was sort of fond of me.

The vows we've registered above
Shall ever cheer and bind me
In constancy to her I love,
The girl I left behind me.

If only he had had a chance to say good-by. Confound this unexpectedly early start! Now he wouldn't even see Sally Ann. She wasn't even on the post. She'd gone riding.

"Forward, ho. Column right, ho." Captain Bone commanded. Trumpeter Shannon rode to his post to the left and rear of the troop commander. As "K" Troop joined the column, General Mackenzie, in the van, was already approaching the gate, where the women of the garrison were waiting.

Out on the prairie there was a flash of white. Peter saw Sally Ann come racing up on her pony. She flung herself out of the saddle and ran to her mother's side. As the staff rode by, Major Lindsay turned out briefly, in accordance with the privilege granted married men in the regiment, to say a last good-by. He leaned from the saddle to kiss his wife and daughter; then trotted back to his place.

My mind her form shall still retain,
In sleeping or in waking,
Until I see my love again,
For whom my heart is breaking.

Peter could perceive now that Sally Ann was wearing a new riding habit of cadet gray. Its long draped skirts made her look at least eighteen. Brass buttons and black and gold braid adorned its close-fitting bodice. A little pillbox cap sat at a cocky angle on brown tresses, tied back with a bow of cavalry yellow. The closer he rode, the more dazzled Peter became.

Now Troop "K" was close to the gate. Sergeant Pinchon, the only married man in its ranks, turned out to bid his wife farewell.

Peter was staring at Sally Ann, his heart in his eyes. In as frank avowal the girl was gazing back, all mystery and shyness gone now. She began beckoning violently. Peter, in a panic, shook his head just as violently.

Captain Bone's voice broke into the pantomime with an

With the fifes carrying clear, "The girl I left behind me."

unprecedented permission: "You may turn out for a moment, Shannon."

Peter automatically obeyed. He rode Justin over to Sally Ann, dismounted and stood there, utterly nonplussed.

All "K" Troop was grinning broadly as it rode by, but they were grins of sentimental sympathy for a lovely girl and a fine-looking young soldier, deep in first love and faced with their first real parting.

" 'Parting,' " First Sergeant Smith quoted to himself, " 'is such sweet sorrow.' "

Sally Ann murmured, "Oh, Pete!" They looked long into each other's eyes. It was as if no one else at all were there. Peter crushed her hands in his. "Sally Ann!"

The Army girl, who had seen troops march off and march back with gaps in the ranks, spoke again. "Take good care of Justin—and yourself. You've both of you got to come back."

"Sure we will, Sally Ann." There was a pause of desperate yearning. Peter, wanting to say many things, was virtually tongue-tied. All he could do was repeat: "Sure we will."

The atmosphere was growing entirely too fervent for Mrs. Lindsay.

"Sally Ann, Peter's troop has passed. He ought to be back at his post," she called.

"Gosh, yes!" Peter, looking after "K" now far ahead, was dismayed. "Good-by, everybody," he shouted, and vaulted into his saddle. Justin, impatient at being left behind, was off like a black streak. Peter thundered up behind his troop commander, like Sheridan saving the day at Winchester. There was smothered laughter in the ranks.

Peter glanced back once. He still could see the little figure in gray frantically waving a handkerchief. The wind wafted last faint strains of band music, the fifes carrying clear.

If ever I should see the day
When Mars shall have resigned me,
For evermore I'd gladly stay
With the girl I left behind me.

18: THRUST OF LANCES

I

ENEMY country, but where was the enemy? Here in the *Llano Estacado*, somewhere in the Staked Plain, was the refuge and stronghold of Chief Quanah Parker and his band of Quohadi Comanches. Yet, though the band comprised hundreds of warriors, with their women and children, and a herd of several thousand ponies, its village could not be found by Mackenzie's scouts.

True, this was a vast area—one hundred thousand square miles—with numerous natural hideouts, timbered hills and unsuspected valleys, but the range of the various hostile bands off reservations was limited by good grazing and hunting grounds. And besides Mackenzie's, two other columns —General Miles' from Fort Dodge and Colonel Davidson with his fine regiment, the Negro 10th Cavalry—were in the field, harrying Kiowas, Comanches, Arapahoes and Cheyennes, who had gone on the warpath.

Still no success crowned Mackenzie's efforts, in spite of the fact that he was using such first-rate scouts as the half-breed Johnson and Seminole-Negroes, expert trailers. With his usual perseverance, the General established a base camp for eight troops of his own regiment and a detachment from the 8th Infantry, escort for the wagon train, and began a thorough scouting of the headwaters of the Brazos, Pecos, and Red rivers. Between forces ranging over that territory, constant communication was maintained by mounted couriers; in the event the Indians were found, the 4th could be rapidly concentrated.

Because Peter had one of the best mounts in the outfit, he was frequently assigned to this communication service—a combination of connecting file and dispatch rider. It was a detail he welcomed. Rides alone across the plains were adventurous. You were on your own and never knew what might turn up. Also, the detail afforded him better opportunity to watch over Justin, since it was necessary always to keep the Morgan horse close at hand for an emergency. Yet, even so, he once found his lariat cut close to the picket pin, and again he discovered that someone had partly severed his cinch-strap; it would have broken at a trot or gallop and given him a bad fall when his saddle turned and dropped off. Obviously, Rick was not letting any chances pass to even scores.

Peter had not the slightest doubt Rick was responsible, though he could not have caught him in the act. Rick was both too smart to be caught and clever enough to make the damage to rope and strap look accidental. Knife marks had not shown, since lariat and strap had been scraped instead of cut. Peter acknowledged he would have been fooled himself if he had not previously made a careful inspection of his equipment.

A certain furtiveness was showing nowadays in Rick's bearing. His old swagger was still there, but there was less of a devil-may-care air to it and more bravado. However, Peter was well aware that the caution enforced on Rick, who knew that most of the troop distrusted him, made the red-haired man more dangerous than ever.

After mess one evening, Peter, himself unobserved, sighted Rick sauntering over to where Justin was picketed. Dusk was falling, and Rick could consider himself more or less unnoticed in the constant movement of troopers in and around the bivouac ground. He moved closer to the horse, speaking soothingly. Justin was wary and backed off as far as his line allowed. He did not like this man in the least. This was the soldier he once had bucked off—who later had whipped him away from the horse herd. Rick continued to come toward him, holding out a hand ingratiatingly, as if to offer something good to eat.

Peter, slow to wrath, felt anger surging up out of his long-stored hatred. This fellow planned to do his beloved Justin some harm. How he could effect it, whether there was some way he could poison the horse, the trumpeter did not know, but he was absolutely positive that Rick could and was about to do his horse serious injury.

Swiftly and truculently Peter pushed in between them. Rick, with a guilty start, jumped back.

"Look, you!" Peter hardly recognized the hoarse, threatening tones as his own voice. "You keep away from my horse—and stay away."

Rick could not squarely meet the younger trooper's eyes, but he spoke up with well-simulated indignation: "What's eatin' you? I was just going to give him a lick of salt."

"Salt nothing! I bet it was arsenic."

"Say, youngster, you'd better button up your lip. I'm not takin'—"

"I told you to stay way from my horse, Rick. And you'll do that or—"

"Aw, go toot your horn! This your private charger? Only a troop horse, ain't he? Mebbe he ain't even that. I heard where a—a rancher had a black Morgan gelding with four white feet stolen off him."

"I guess it's a *Comanchero,* not a rancher, you're talking about, Rick. That's who hit me over the head and took my horse. And my horse got away from the herd the night you were on guard. I'll swear there's some kind of a hook-up between you and old Tafoya."

"You lie! Try and prove that—and see what happens to you."

"I'll prove it first chance I get. In the meantime, you let my horse alone or I'll—"

Rick gave vent to a sarcastic laugh. "Or you'll what?" he demanded. "Kinda threatenin', ain't you? Or you'll what?"

Husky and hardened by his more than two years with the regiment, Peter walked slowly toward the other, doubling his fists.

"Or I'll beat your face in," he answered. "Now or any time."

"Oh, no you won't." Rick's hand darted down to the butt of his revolver.

Peter stood still and regarded him with a level stare.

"Bluff, Rick. You wouldn't dare shoot me right here in the middle of the outfit," he declared.

"Wouldn't I? I'd drill you right through the heart. By the time they run up, I'd have your own gun jerked out and leave it lay beside the body. My story is you pulled down on me—they all know you hate my guts—and I shot first. Self-defense sure enough, Shannon. How's that hit you?"

"More bluff," said Peter, moving up closer. "Put up your fists."

Bluff it had been, but shame and the instinct of a cornered gunman suddenly crystallized it into deadly intent. Rick's fingers closed around the butt of his Colt to whip it from its holster in a long-practiced, fast draw.

Peter saw the murderous light in the man's eyes. For an instant he half recoiled. Then his muscles tensed for a jump and a grab at that gun arm, though he knew that any action of his, however swift, would be too late.

Half-drawn, the revolver slid back into its holster. Rick uttered a smothered shriek of anguish. His face contorted. Both his hands went behind him, clutching his rear.

Decidedly Justin did not like that fellow. The horse had taken advantage of opportunity as it presented itself and nipped the fellow sharply in the buttocks.

Gazing after the retreating Rick, who was holding together the shredded seat of his breeches, Justin emitted a ringing snort of satisfaction. As plain as words, it said: "Served him right. He had that coming to him."

II

Under a dark sky threatening rain, Peter was riding communications between his troop and squadron headquarters when he saw another horseman approaching. At considerable distance he recognized his friend, Corporal Elliot. Elliot was carrying the guidon, cased. Ordinarily, if assigned to carry dispatches, he would have left it at troop headquarters.

The two reined in abreast and greeted each other affectionately.

Elliot said: "One of the Seminoles has found a wagon-train trail. Probably doesn't amount to anything. Reckon it must be immigrants. Sure do take their chances coming through Comanche country. But Captain Bone thought the General ought to know about it. Rushed me off in such a hurry I had to bring along the stick. No place to leave it." He swung the guidon in its stirrup socket.

"I'll report to the Cap'n I passed you on the way," Peter said.

"Do that, Pete." Lance smiled briefly at him and rode off at a steady gallop.

Peter, riding in the opposite direction, turned in the saddle to gaze after him. He was worried about his friend. In the past days Lance had been more deeply sunken than usual in morose brooding. The prospect of action had not revived him as it usually did. Although his comrade would talk little, Peter thought he understood the reasons for his melancholy. The one-time Confederate cavalryman still mourned a lost leader, a lost cause, a vanished golden age. The South he had loved was gone, and his mourning for it now had become an accustomed ache. But learning of its present fate at the hands of the Carpetbaggers caused new and almost unbearable bitterness. Peter half-expected that some day Lance might desert and go home to throw away his life in some desperate, quixotic action.

Still looking back and wondering anxiously how he could help him, Peter saw Lance halt suddenly at the mouth of a draw, saw him begin to beckon urgently. He whirled Justin and urged him into a dead gallop. Before he could come up, Elliot had disappeared into the draw.

Peter turned in and brought his mount to a sudden stop. He would never forget the tableau that met his eyes—staged within the frame of the wall of the draw.

Not far in front of him Lance sat his horse, immobile. Facing him, some hundreds of yards down the draw, a Comanche chieftain, splendid in eagle-feather war bonnet and brilliant war paint, sat his pony, equally motionless. Even at that distance Peter recognized the fierce visage, indelibly imprinted in his mind since Trooper Gregg died that day in Canyon Blanco. It was Quanah Parker. The chief carried a small, round shield of painted bull's hide. His right hand grasped a long lance, just as Elliot's grasped the guidon. At Quanah's rear was a single, mounted warrior.

The two Comanches seemed on the point of flight, expecting the two cavalrymen to be followed by more. But when no others appeared, the Indians, reluctant to risk a shot in the back as they ran, did not move.

"Peter," Lance Elliot called back over his shoulder. "Don't shoot. I'm going to keep those two here as long as I can. If I can hold 'em a while, then chase and trail 'em, we can locate the village. When I charge, get out of here and get the word to Mackenzie fast."

"I'm not leaving you, Lance."

"You are." The words were stern. "That's an order."

The Indians watched with eager curiosity that held them in place, while Corporal Elliot lifted the ferrule of the guidon from the stirrup socket, lowered it to the ground and slipped off the casing. The red and white flag fluttered free. He grasped the guidon lance midway in its nine-foot length. Dipped the gleaming metal spearpoint on its end forward as in executing the guidon salute. Gripped the lance firmly with right hand and beneath right arm. Laid his reins on his horse's neck for a moment to raise his left hand toward his brow in a strange gesture. That, thought Peter suddenly, is how knights lowered the vizors of their helmets before combat.

What he next saw amazed him even more. Quanah was also lowering the point of the long lance he carried.

The cavalryman and the Comanche, lances leveled, spurred their horses toward each other in a headlong charge.

III

When those few vivid moments flashed back into his mind, as they would all his life, Peter was again affected by the strange sentiment that he had witnessed a scene taken straight out of the 5th Century for re-enactment in the 19th. Old Sir Thomas Malory might well have described it in his book of King Arthur and his noble knights of the Round Table. "And they gat their spears and dressed them," he might have written. "Then straightway the Blue Knight and the Red Knight did battle, hurtling together on horseback, coming together as the thunder. Above the clash of arms the herald of the tourney blew his trumpet, loud and shrill."

The agony of his indecision that day long would obsess Peter, too. What should he have done? He had definite orders from Corporal Elliot, his superior. It was his duty to reach General Mackenzie as soon as possible with the vital intelligence that Quanah had been found. Yet, how could he desert a friend, his first in the regiment and his best, leaving him to fight it out against odds of two to one?

He started reaching for his carbine. But Lance had ordered him specifically not to shoot. Instead, Peter found himself raising his trumpet to his lips. Its long-carrying tones might bring troops quicker than the report of a carbine. With all the strength of his lungs he sounded the *Flourish* and then *Attention.*

Even as Peter sounded off, the horsemen were drawing together at top speed. Elliot handled the heavy ashen guidon effortlessly, holding it unswervingly as he had the light lance with which he had won ring tilts at home before the War. Its flag whipped out like a banneret borne into battle. Even under that lowering sky, its spearpoint gleamed.

And against him galloped Quanah Parker in all his barbaric panoply. How superb his horsemanship was! He rode without reins, his legs guiding his spirited war pony. Red hands grasped shield and long lance, held as steadily as Elliot's, its point full on his adversary's heart.

Elliot and Parker. Old English names, Quanah's from his captive white mother. Perhaps ancestors of these two had charged down on one another in a tournament at King Arthur's Camelot.

Peter was utterly unable to move. Helpless, fascinated, he watched the impact of the charge. He saw the timed skill with which Quanah with his shield deflected Elliot's spearpoint so that it sped by his left side—saw the terrible emergence of the Comanche's reddened lance point under the cavalryman's left shoulder blade—saw Lance reel out of his saddle.

Justin let his rider see nothing more. The Morgan whirled of his own accord and dashed out of the draw. It was only in the nick of time. Both Comanches were riding down on the surviving trooper, blazing away with their revolvers. Peter felt his right ear sting sharply, but other shots went wide, and the Indians did not pursue him out on to the prairie.

IV

Mackenzie, as soon as he received Peter's report, pushed out scouting parties. But all their careful searching was in vain. Rain and rocky ground foiled efforts to pick up the trail of Quanah and his companion. The fact that they had been seen in the vicinity was of high importance, however. The Comanche village Mackenzie was seeking could not be very far away.

Sadly, a detail from Troop "K" buried their guidon-bearer. First Sergeant Sam Smith gazed down on the grave. Peter Shannon, his face working, stood beside him.

"His time had come," the big man said softly, "and it was a gallant way of going out—one Lance would have chosen."

They were in enemy country. The traditional three volleys could not be fired over the grave, nor could *Taps* be sounded, even if Peter had been able to master himself and blow that farewell. There was no chaplain present with the command. The First Sergeant recited some of the burial service from memory: " 'I am the Resurrection and the Life, saith the Lord. He that believeth in Me, though he were dead, yet shall he live. And whosoever liveth and believeth in Me, shall never die.' "

Moved by the same impulse, the sergeant and the trumpeter saluted the grave of their comrade.

Helpless, he watched the impact of the charge

There was no time to linger. Walking over to remount, Smith's foot struck an object that rang. It was Quanah's steel lance, left on the field of battle. He picked it up and examined it wonderingly.

"Look here," he called. "This is an antique Spanish lance. Once it must have been wielded by some captain or man-at-arms who marched with Cortez in the conquest of the Aztecs. And now, three centuries later, in the hands of a Comanche, heir to part of the Aztec empire, it has slain one of us who come to conquer." He stood musing for a moment, then spoke softly:

" 'There are more things in heaven and earth, Horatio, than are dreamt of in your philosophy.' "

19: DEPTHS OF THE EARTH

I

José Pieda Tafoya had fallen into Mackenzie's hands at last. The trail of the wagon-train, reported by scouts and supposed to be that of immigrants, proved to be the *Comanchero's* when a troop followed it up.

The General himself, promptly notified, arrived at a gallop. Evidently he considered this capture important, for he made no attempt to conceal his satisfaction.

"Got you at last, Tafoya," Mackenzie snapped. "You devil, you've sold your last gun to Indians to kill soldiers."

Tafoya shrugged his plump shoulders and spoke volubly in Spanish.

"Says he can't speak English, sir," Major Lindsay translated. "Claims he's an innocent trader named Perez. Lies, of course. I can identify him myself. This is José Pieda Tafoya all right."

Mackenzie scowled blackly. "I don't doubt it. But get some more who know him. Send for Sergeant Charlton and young Shannon—he saw him recently. I don't want *Señor* Tafoya to die thinking it was all a case of mistaken identity. Also, Lindsay, get hold of the nearest supply wagon."

The Sergeant and Peter arrived to identify the trader eagerly and angrily.

The General nodded. "That's good enough. Now, Tafoya, there's just one thing can save your neck. Tell me where Quanah's hideout is."

Tafoya looked up uncomprehendingly. *"No sabe,"* he said.

"He and his band—probably a good many lodges of the Kiowas, too—are holed up somewhere in this vicinity. I know that. Only yesterday we had a brush with Quanah himself. Sooner or later I'll root 'em out. Is it worth that worthless life of yours to save me time?"

"No sabe," stubbornly insisted *Señor* Tafoya.

"Last chance. Tell me where those Indians are or I'll hang you higher than Haman."

Not one of the listening cavalrymen doubted Mackenzie meant what he said. He would bother with no formal trial. He had all the evidence he required that the death of many a soldier and settler was on the *Comanchero's* head.

But Tafoya still muttered *"No sabe,"* and there was even insolence in his voice. Hang him? Where? The plains stretched away for miles, with never a tree in sight.

Mackenzie barked orders. The teamster of the wagon sent for, unhitched his mules. The wagon tongue, propped up, became an adequate gallows tree. One end of a hemp rope was run through its staple, and several troopers laid hold of it. A noose, made on the other end, was adjusted around Tafoya's squat neck.

Now terror began to show in the back of his eyes, but it was less of this death, which he still doubted the General would carry through, than of another. Tafoya knew with direct certainty that if he betrayed the hiding place of the Indians, Quanah would never rest till he caught him and broiled him alive.

"String him up," Mackenzie ordered.

The fat trader's feet left the ground. The knot of the noose cut into the folds of flesh at the back of his neck, and his own weight inexorably tightened it.

Peter, watching, could feel no great pity. He laid a hand protectingly on Justin's mane and thought: Now he'll never get you.

Tafoya was swinging now. A scream burst from his nearly throttled windpipe.

"Por Cristo, let me down! I tell."

"Slack off, men," ordered General Mackenzie.

Tafoya told—and told the truth. Once scouts had verified his information, he was released. Driven by dread of Quanah, the trader fled, never stopping until he reached the Rockies. There he spent the rest of his life, befriended by a man whose cattle he once had stolen. He never dared return to the Staked Plain.

II

Sergeant Charlton and a scout detachment, following Tafoya's directions, reined in suddenly on the edge of a deep and utterly unsuspected abyss. Before them yawned the canyon of Palo Duro, the most secret and cherished hiding place of the Kiowas and Comanches. The awed troopers stared down into those dizzy depths where Indians, ponies, and lodges looked like tiny miniatures. An eagle swooping above them seemed no larger than a sparrow.

Charlton swung away. He had seen enough. "Gallop, ho," he commanded. They galloped hard to report to Mackenzie.

Sunrise, September 27, 1874. The head of the 4th Cavalry's column halted at the canyon rim, where a narrow trail led down into the depths.

General Mackenzie turned to the lieutenant commanding the leading troop. "Mr. Thompson," he ordered quietly, "take your men down and open the fight."

Troop "K's" turn came. Captain Bone dismounted his men. "Follow me," he commanded and, leading his charger, disappeared over the rim. Peter was next. With Justin following, he took a deep breath and stepped forward. It was only a goat track, that trail, narrow and zigzagging. Over its edge was a drop of some seven hundred feet. Peter flattened himself against the canyon wall, clinging to it as his boots slid and slipped. The line of troopers ahead of him wound downward like a long, blue snake. Behind him it must be the same, but he could not risk looking back. Justin's nervous snortings rustled the hair on the top of his head. The sure-footed Morgan would not slip—his master was confident of that. Yet if some trooper or horse higher up the trail lost his footing, he would sweep the men and animals in front of them over the edge. Peter's stomach knotted up, and sweat ran down his backbone. And if the Indians caught them here, strung out on this trail—

But the van had reached the bottom before a sentinel warrior discovered them and whooped the alarm. Too late! The leading troop deployed and went into action, covering the descent of the remainder of the regiment.

The canyon rang to yells and shouts. Up the gorge boiled Comanches and Kiowas. Volleys blasted them back. Sharpshooters picked off Indian snipers, firing from ledges along the canyon walls. Each troop, as it reached the bottom, formed up and mounted. "E" and "K" stretched in line across the canyon floor. General Mackenzie rode out in front of them, and Peter, catching his shout and signal, sounded the *Charge*. Its brazen notes were still echoing as they galloped into the billowing powder smoke.

They charged down the valley in a running fight, firing from the saddle. Mounted warriors, swarming out of the side ravines to meet them, were swept back by the blue wave. Pushed hard though they were, the red horsemen's retreat was stubborn. While the sun rose blindingly behind them, they turned to fire back at their pursuers.

Past lodge after lodge drove the charge. Squaws and children fled down the gullies. Braves, trying to recover their squealing war ponies, were ridden over. The 4th was taking its casualties, too, but remarkably few. Peter saw the trumpeter of another troop double over his pommel, shot through the stomach. The old soldier Persimmons took a bullet between his eyes and plunged down into the dust. He had his release at last.

Three miles they had charged. Far enough. Fours to the left about. Gallop. They fought their way back.

Troops behind them had set the snug winter camp on fire, along with its vast quantities of supplies: robes, kettles, buffalo meat, and flour and sugar issued by the Government to the Indians before they left their reservations for the warpath.

Mackenzie had won an easy victory, his casualties extremely light. Boldness and willingness to take heavy risks, when they seemed justified, had achieved it. The enemy never had recovered from the first shock of surprise. Smashing, hell-for-leather charges had given the Indians little chance to rally. The red man, valiant in swooping attack, seldom was capable of dogged, last-ditch defense. And the cavalry had early captured the bulk of the Indians' pony herd. Dismounted, the plains Indians were almost helpless.

When the 4th emerged from Palo Duro, it marched away with a moving hollow square in its center. Each side was formed by a troop in column; its front and rear by troops in line. It was a living corral. Within it were the captured horses of the Indians—fourteen hundred and fifty of them.

III

The next morning, Peter Shannon heard the grimmest orders of his Army career. General Mackenzie had ruled that the captured ponies must be destroyed at once. One troop was detailed to slaughter them; another—"K"—to drag the carcasses together in a heap.

First Sergeant Smith spared a few minutes to talk to Peter, for there was a look of desperation almost on the young trooper's face.

"Trumpeter, we're obeying orders," he declared firmly. "And you'll do your part with the rest of the outfit." The big man's look softened. "Don't try to tell me you're any fonder of horses than I am," he went on. "It's heart-breaking duty. We can thank God we don't have to do the shooting.

"Yes, I know, Peter, we share the responsibility. It lies on my soul—the fine horses that have died in mankind's wars. In the Civil War, the Union Army, just to replace horse casualties, needed more than five hundred *a day*."

"But, Sergeant, we don't have to shoot these horses. We could herd 'em north and turn 'em over to the Remount or ranchers."

"Look here, lad. Have you forgotten already what happened at Canyon Blanco? Before we reached Fort Griffin, which is a good two hundred miles, the Comanches would attack, stampede the herd and run off all their own horses and a bunch of ours.

"The General's order is absolutely justified, tough as it is. Once the Indians find themselves on the prairie without mounts, they won't be able to get back to the reservations fast enough to ask for peace on any terms. Unlimber your lariat and come on."

Peter stood by, sick and shaking, trying not to watch, while the shots cracked mercilessly. There was some slight consolation in the knowledge that some of the horses had been spared. Troopers who had lost their own mounts, along with Johnson and the other scouts, had been allowed to take their pick. But many a splendid animal was being slaughtered.

" 'K' Troop keep well over to the right," the First Sergeant called. "Keep well out of the line of fire or somebody'll get hit."

Obeying, Peter dismounted. He felt sick. He patted Justin and leaned on him, head and arms resting on the saddle.

Off to one side of the milling pony herd, Private Rick

grunted with satisfaction. Taking cover behind his own horse, he raised his carbine. His target had obligingly lined itself up for him. There, nice and still, stood Shannon and his nag—just waiting for it.

This was plain bull luck. Rick was about to desert, but he had craved urgently to settle this account before he left. Now the same confusion which would make it easy for him to slip away and go over the hill was masking his revenge for him. It would be the most evident kind of an accident, with all this wild shooting of ponies going on.

At three hundred yards, it was a fairly easy shot. The way Shannon's head was drooping over the saddle, Rick figured he could drill him through the skull and the nag through the spine with one shot. Talk about 'two birds with one stone,' thought Rick, chuckling to himself.

He sighted carefully. He did not forget his breath hold and his trigger squeeze. *Crack!* His shot merged with the general fusillade. Rick, pausing only to see both man and horse go down in a heap, slipped swiftly away.

Living the hunted, haunted life of a deserter from the United States Army, Rick never learned that his shot had not been the brilliant success he believed. A fairly stiff breeze had been blowing that day, and he had forgotten his windage.

The bullet had missed Peter's skull. He sprang up unharmed.

But the black Morgan horse lay where he had fallen. His four white feet twitched and were still.

20: SOLDIER'S FAREWELL

I

PETER SHANNON, chief trumpeter, Troop "K," 4th U. S. Cavalry, was standing his last retreat. Squadrons in line, the regiment stretched across the parade ground, a gallant sight. Ranks stood almost immobile, except where here and there a troop horse stamped or tossed his head. The rays of a setting sun burnished brighter the polished instruments of the band and massed trumpeters.

Yonder, at the Commanding Officer's quarters, brilliant-hued silk gleamed. Sergeants were bringing out the national and regimental standards, uncasing them, mounting up. Flanked by color guards, a two-platoon escort riding in front and rear, the standards approached the waiting regiment.

Mackenzie's voice rang out: "Draw sabres. Escort halt." The standards came on until they were fifty paces in front of the General.

"Present sabres." The long, blue ranks were suddenly a field of flashing steel—blades whipped from scabbards and upward in salute. As the sabres rose, the guidons dipped in homage, and Sergeant Wills and his massed trumpeters sounded *To the Standard.*

His trumpet returned to the carry, Peter sat his horse rigidly while the band played *The Star-Spangled Banner,* and the garrison flag fluttered slowly down its staff. As always, there was a catch in his throat and a throbbing in his pulses. Those majestic strains of music, the sight of Old Glory—they made you feel things about your country, things you used just to take for granted. Silently, Peter made a vow. If I ever begin to forget my love for my country and all I owe her, he promised himself, I'll go to an Army post some evening when they're standing Retreat. I'll take off my civilian hat and hold it against my left breast, the way civilians salute, and listen to the Anthem and watch the Flag come down. And then I'll remember.

His last Retreat. His time was up, his discharge waiting at Headquarters. John Shannon had adamantly refused to allow his son to re-enlist. Peter must come home and go to college. Yet, how could he leave this fine regiment of his, with all it meant to him. . . . Take off the blue uniform with its cavalry-yellow stripes he wore so proudly. . . .

Leave behind the good comrades with whom he served and the valiant memory of those he had seen die in battle?

The troop rode off the parade ground to stand stables. Deeply despondent, Peter dismounted. As he led off, he gently stroked his mount's forehead.

"Got to leave you, too," he said softly and sadly. "And I thought that day on the Plains that you had left me."

Justin affectionately nuzzled his master's cheek.

II

The veterinary had explained to Peter what had happened that day of the pony slaughter, when the wind of a bullet had fanned his hair, and the black Morgan horse had collapsed and lain as if dead.

" 'Creasing,' the old-timers call it," the veterinary declared. "It was a trick the wild horse hunters used. When they were after an especially fine mustang and couldn't run him down and rope him or catch him in any other way, they tried creasing as a last resort. A very carefully placed shot through the upper portion of the neck, just in front of the withers, would severe a nerve and cause temporary paralysis. While the cayuse lay there stunned, the hunters galloped up and roped and double-hobbled him before he came to.

"From all I hear, it worked about once out of fifty tries. Cruel trick, creasing. Must have killed a good many fine horses.

"Not that I believe anybody was trying to crease your mount, Shannon. Don't figure it was an accident, either. Somebody was taking a pot shot at you. I hear tell a certain trooper in your outfit deserted the same day. And that wasn't what you'd call in highfallutin' lingo 'a mere coincidence.' "

Peter had completely agreed. Good riddance, Rick.

Now, finishing a last, loving grooming of Justin's sleek, black hide, he banged down brush and currycomb in sudden, angry resolution.

Leave the Army? Leave his best girl? Sally Ann was an Army girl and always would be and leaving the Service was just the same as giving her up for good. Leave his horse, this beloved mount of his, to be turned into troop herd, even though the stable sergeant had assured him that Justin would be assigned to a good rider and a kind master?

Mouth grimly set, Peter stamped off to the orderly room.

III

First Sergeant Sam Smith sat behind his rough table and calmly heard out the rush of eager, vehement words.

"I *won't* go!" Peter avowed. "I'm staying in the Army. If they won't let me re-up in this outfit, I'll change my name and age and enlist in another."

Quietly the Top answered:

"Steady there, Peter. Look forward a bit. What's ahead of you? A commission maybe? Not for years. Congress is cutting the Army down even further. We never learn. All the senior officers for years will be the Civil War veterans we have now. The shavetails—all there are vacancies for—will come from West Point.

"Want to stay in the ranks all your life? To what end? Some day our people will look on a good soldier as one following an honorable career, as worthy of respect. They don't now. For the trooper who stays in the Service, his destiny is either a lonely grave in the prairie or a cheerless bunk in an Old Soldier's Home.

"Get your education. I've taken you as far as I can. Then

come back to the Army if you want to—via West Point or from civil life."

Peter's stubborn determination began to ebb. It could not be otherwise, his admiration, his almost worshipful reverence for the high character and wisdom of this man being what they were.

Sam Smith smiled. "There may be a couple more immediate matters on your mind, making you hate to leave. There's a certain young lady on this post—we will not, of course, bandy about a lady's name—who has just been given a horse of her own by her father. A troop horse bought from the Government. A black horse, by the by, with four white feet."

Peter's eyes lit up. "Sergeant, you mean—"

"Wait! It was told me in confidence that the young lady wanted the horse as a keepsake of a young trooper who used to ride him. She said, I am reliably informed, that though the trooper might never come back just to see her, he certainly would to see his horse."

IV

Peter Shannon, honorably discharged after serving one enlistment with character "Excellent" in the U. S. Cavalry, stowed his baggage in the Concord wagon that would leave in half an hour for a long night drive to the railroad. General Mackenzie's parting praise and that of his own troop officers and the cordial hand-clasps of his comrades-in-arms had filled him with a warm glow.

Presenting himself at the Lindsay quarters, he was received by the Adjutant and his wife. Peter was offering his heartfelt thanks for the Major's purchase of Justin when Sally Ann made her entrance.

She had on a new dress. In its making had collaborated *Godey's Lady Book,* one of Mr. Buttrick's best patterns, skilled sempstress work by Mrs. Lindsay and Ma Simmons, and more of the Major's pay than he liked. Peter could only have reported that it was yellow silk—cavalry yellow—and that there were bows and lace and things here and there. But such inadequate observation mattered not at all, since the dress achieved the desired effect. Sally Ann, stepping in with hoop skirts swaying, her brown hair put up and wreathed by a chaplet of marigolds, was undeniably a vision.

"Gosh!" exclaimed Peter in sincerest tribute.

"Sally Ann, the dress seems to be a success," her mother smilingly observed.

Out on the porch, in the soft air of a Texan spring, Peter was having a difficult time saying good-by. He was managing it very poorly when the first notes of *Taps* sounded. They were sounding it in harmony and with an echo—that, Peter realized, was Sergeant Wills' send-off for him.

Softly Sally Ann began to sing, as the lovely call was repeated.

> *"Love, good-night.*
> *Must you go*
> *When the day*
> *And the night*
> *Need you so?*
> *Though we part,*
> *Ever rest*
> *In my heart."*

That was enough for Peter as, indeed, it ought to have been enough for any man. He took the girl in his arms and held her close. The trim little form under the smooth silk felt at once firm and yielding. Her face was upturned, the way it had been in the dream that time, and her eyes were shining up into his.

"Sally Ann," he whispered, "remember how you said that *Taps* was like someone you loved dearly saying good-night?"

She nodded. Her fragrance was all about him, as he bent and kissed her, and her lips answered his.

"Oh!" a small voice said breathlessly and tremulously.

"Sally Ann, do you know what that means?" Peter, breathless, too, but sternly serious, demanded. "It means you'll wait for me."

"It just couldn't mean anything else, Pete."

"They'll say we're still awf'ly young. They'll say it's silly and we don't know our own minds and that we'll forget."

"It isn't 'they.' It's you and me, Pete, and I'll wait for you—always."

"I'll be back as soon as I can," he promised. "Good-by, Sally Ann."

They kissed again, their young hearts beating fast. Peter ran down the steps, turned once to wave and was gone in the night.

Down in "K" Troop stables another good-by was said. A trooper's arms were around his horse's sturdy neck, his face buried in a black mane. There were gentle snortings and a sound that was suspiciously like a quickly-suppressed sob.

A comradely slap on a sleek haunch. " 'By, Justin," in a gruff voice. Steps hurrying out. Then the crack of a driver's

"Don't take it so hard, hoss. He'll be back."

whip and the rattle of wagon wheels.

From the stable came a shrill, yearning neigh. The stable guard halted his pacing and called:

"Don't take it so hard, hoss. He'll be back."

AUTHOR'S AFTERWORD

General Mackenzie, one of the ablest officers in the Old Army that fought our Indian wars, is drawn from life. Mention is made of Lt. Robert G. Carter and of Sergeant Charlton, whose books on the 4th Cavalry's Texas campaigns were principal sources. Most of the other characters are fictional, although the sabre instructor, Sergeant Pinchon, echoes—almost verbatim—sentiments once expressed by a young sabre enthusiast who later became a tank expert: the late Gen. George S. Patton, Jr.

The dog, Old Taylor, and the horse, Big Bill, were borrowed from the 6th Cavalry.

A statue to Justin Morgan, progenitor of the Morgan horses, was not erected until 1921.

Except that Troop "K" is credited with participating in actions where it was not present, the 4th Cavalry's campaigns are sketched with a fair measure of fidelity. Those interested may find it worthwhile to consult a painstaking map compiled by E. D. Dorchester: Trails and routes used by the 4th U. S. Cavalry under command of Gen. R. S. Mackenzie in its operations against hostile Indians in Texas, Indian-Territory (now Oklahoma), New Mexico, and Old Mexico during the period of 1871–75; Freeport, Tex., 1927. A copy will be found in the map room of the New York Public Library.